GRUESOME TWOSOME

Keith Brumpton

■SCHOLASTIC

Scholastic Children's Books,
Euston House, 24 Eversholt Street,
London NW1 1DB, UK
a division of Scholastic UK Ltd
London ~ New York ~ Toronto ~ Sydney ~ Auckland
Mexico City ~ New Delhi ~ Hong Kong

First published by Scholastic UK Ltd, 2005

ISBN 0 439 96858 5

Printed by Nørhaven Paperback A/S, Denmark

Dedicated to John Gorman,
from whose imagination much of this sprung.

FOR ONE NIGHT ONLY!

MACABRE'S CIRCUS

THRILLS & SPILLS FOR ALL THE FAMILY!!!

SEE THE GREAT MACABRE AND HIS LIONS!
LAUGH AT THE CRAZY CLOWNS!
GASP AT THE GRUESOME TWOSOME!
THRILL TO THE SIGHT OF THE DANCING PENGUINS!
THE WITCH, BADHAGG, WILL BE THERE TO READ YOUR FORTUNE

CANDYFLOSS
TOFFEE APPLES
ICE COLD DRINKS

PERFORMANCE BEGINS 19.30
LATECOMERS WILL BE PUNISHED

GRUESOME TWOSOME

A spine-tingling tale for children who don't mind having their spines tingled. . .

MESSRS HOMBURG & HOMBURG, SOLICITORS

The events in this story took place in the past. But do not for one moment think that the Great Macabre and his Circus have vanished for ever. On the contrary, they might appear in your neighbourhood at any time. If and when that day comes, you, dear reader, must be ready. Please take it from us, who witnessed these events at first hand, that not all circuses are fun, and not all clowns wish to make you laugh. Be vigilant!

Joshua T Homburg

MESSRS J AND L HOMBURG,
SOLICITORS,
FOGHORN FALLS
NOVEMBER 12TH, 19—

CHAPTER ONE

A Performance

The circus tent was pitched in the middle of a windswept, muddy field, just a few miles from town.

On either side of the field stood two jagged, twisted, oak trees, whose weird silhouettes suggested they must recently have been struck by lightning. A thin, damp mist was coiling itself a few inches above the frozen ground. In one week's time it would be Halloween. . .

For several months now, this same circus had been travelling from town to town: Foghorn Falls, Darkwood, Dogstooth; the circus had called at each of them in turn. At first the crowds were healthy, for in truth there weren't many other attractions in this part of the world. But just lately, the Great Macabre and his Circus had been playing to empty tents.

There were lots of reasons why this might be. The weather had turned bad. People were getting ready for Halloween. And then there was the escaped lion. Having a wild man-eating beast on the loose never did much for business. . .

3

THE
DOGSTOOTH COURIER
Wild beast still at large!

An African lion, believed to be the same recently escaped from Macabre's Travelling Circus, was yesterday spotted in the high street of Dogstooth (pop: 204). After a brief disturbance in Kerogan's Gentlemen's Barbers, the creature (believed to be highly dangerous), ran off. The public are warned to be on their guard.

But the likeliest reason for the thin crowds was the fact that Macabre's circus was no longer what it once had been. Most of the performers, like the Big Top itself, had seen better days, and no amount of giant posters or razzmattazz could change that.

Around the ring, row upon row of rickety wooden seats lay empty. There didn't seem much point in the silver-suited circus band striking up, but strike up they did.

Olga the Bearded Lady counted just four heads in the audience, which was odd because she had sold five tickets. She noted with alarm that one of the mangy old lions was licking its lips with a satisfied look.

There were two small children seated in the front row, then, behind them, a lady with elaborately shaped bluegrey hair, and a short, balding man.

TCHING, TCHING, TCHING!

A trio of brightly dressed seals began playing the cymbals, whilst a red-nosed clown called Mr Spangly blew a loud, tuneless fanfare on his trumpet. Into the

4

sawdust ring strode the Great Macabre, Ringmaster. He was a terrifying figure to behold, with his white face, green teeth and rustling cape, blackasbat'swing.

"Lllladies and gentleman! Sssssmall children!" he bellowed. "Please accept my welcome to the grrrreatest circus in the world!"

TCHING!

Macabre threw a look, sharp as a dagger, in the direction of the poor seal who'd been so careless as to drop its cymbal in the middle of his speech.

If truth be told, the circus band weren't very good. But what they lacked in ability they certainly made up for in volume. To the accompaniment of blazing trumpets and crashing cymbals, Madame Mimi and her Performing Poodles raced into the ring.

"Rowf-rowf, rowf-rowf, rowf-rowf!"

To an untrained eye, the poodles seemed out of control. Eyes flashing and teeth bared, they sprinted across the sawdust in a growling frenzy. Madame Mimi, with her bright red cheeks and lipstick, appeared powerless to control them let alone get them to perform.

The crowd (if you can call four people a crowd), leaned nervously forward on their seats, sensing that all was not well. As it turned out, tricks would indeed be performed, but not by the poodles. . .

Whilst Macabre watched scowling from the ring-side, the hapless Madame Mimi soon found herself surrounded by a pack of snarling canines. To avoid their razorsharp teeth, the frightened trainer began running towards a flaming hoop in the middle of the ring. She leaped through it and then through another. Someone in the crowd laughed. The poodles were still in pursuit and Madame Mimi now found sanctuary balanced on top of a huge drum. She began running on the drum, running to stay above those snapping incisors – the drum rolled round the ring, poodles in pursuit – it was almost impressive.

"Mum, I thought the poodles performed, not the lady," said Hercules Inkblot to his mother.

Macabre's expression grew dark as thundercloud. He strode into the ring with his whip and brought Madame Mimi's act to an abrupt conclusion. The lady in question fled backstage, still pursued by her crazed poodles.

"Rowf-rowf, rowf-rowf!"

"Lllladies annnn gentlemen! Little kiddytots!" announced Macabre. "If you value your lives, please welcome warmly the strongest man in the world, arms of iron, fists of steel, please greet the Remarkable Otto!"

A giant of a man clad in a moth-eaten leopardskin leotard advanced uneasily into the ring. His long handlebar moustache could not conceal a worried frown, and this anxiety seemed at once to reach the small audience scattered beneath the big tent. A nervous silence hung in the air. Howlingwind ruffled the upper reaches of the tent.

The Remarkable Otto had in front of him a huge iron bar. It was as thick as the axle of a steam train.

And it seemed beyond imagining that any human could lift such a thing, let alone bend it like a party balloon.

"I vill now bend ze metal bar." The Remarkable Otto gestured with his muscled arm and one of the clowns began a loud, stuttering drum roll.

Though unquestionably strong, Otto was also very nervous, and crowds made his condition worse. Even small crowds. He threw a glance in the direction of the top-hatted Macabre and what he saw there did not fill his frame with any confidence either . . . a coldstare.

"Why doesn't he *do* something?" whispered young Master Inkblot seated in row G.

The Remarkable Otto flexed his arms and felt the cold sweat gathering on his forehead begin to trickle downwards. Silence rushed around him like a wave.

"Aaaaaumph!" he gasped, tugging on the iron bar. The metal weight refused to budge. It seemed the strongman couldn't lift it, let alone bend it. Red-faced, growing more anxious, he licked his lips.

"Aaaaaumph!" The Remarkable Otto's biceps bulged once more, but still the bar would not move. The Great Macabre gave a signal and the circus band burst back into life. Under cover of darkness (for the lights had been dimmed), the strongman hurried off stage, head bowed, not daring to glance left or right for fear of catching the eye of you-know-who.

Two small children in white leotards watched him

go. Palefaced and darkeyed, they wanted to offer words of encouragement but the Remarkable Otto did not pause on his way from the tent.

"Us next," said the older of the twins.

His sister smiled and bit her lip.

Back inside, Macabre bestrode the ring once more, black-booted, top-hatted, eyes aflame.

"Ladies and children, gentle – mannn, please pray SILENCE – for the amazing – the death-defying – the awe-inspiring – Gruesome Twosome!"

The lights went down. And into the ring ran two very small and odd-looking children. Cuthbert and Fatima were their names, but everyone in the circus knew them as the "Gruesome Twosome". They were the stars of this tawdry show, the only act who could bring the crowd to its feet. The other performers acknowledged the fact with bad grace, as did the Great Macabre. Jealousy is a terrible emotion. It eats into everything. And it had eaten into Macabre's dark heart like nothing else. The more dependent he became on the Gruesome Twosome, the more he hated them. It was a blind, irrational hate, gnawing away at him as the beetles had gnawed away at the mouldy canvas of the big top.

At the sight of the Gruesome Twosome, the applause of the sparse crowd echoed round the tent like the slap of seal flippers.

MY TRIP TO THE CIRCUS
By Hercules Inkblot (aged 8)

When mother said we were going to the circus I was very happy because I like circuses. But when we got there I didn't like it because they played bad music and the man with the mustash was nasty to everyone. The only thing I liked was the candyfloss and the Gruesome Twosome. They throw knives and do tricks and they are very brave even though they are only young like about my age. Next time mother says we can go to a movie instead, circuses are too frightening.

Two kids, white as chalk and frail as wheat-chaff, tumbling across the ring. Fleet of foot. Lightning fast. At last the audience came to life. Spotlights criss-crossed the arena whilst Cuthbert juggled a set of silversharp knives and Fatima back-flipped in time to the music. She cartwheeled over to the "Wheel of Death", a large rotating disc painted in the colours of the rainbow.

Next, a clown tied a blindfold over Cuthbert's eyes as a second clown fixed Fatima to the rainbow-coloured wheel. The metal clamps around her wrists sprang into place and from that moment on there could be no escape. . . Drumroll!

The lights were dimmed and a sudden silence descended amidst the sawdust and canvas. Even little Hercules Inkblot was transfixed.

9

All eyes were now on Cuthbert. Blindfold, he turned towards his sister, knife poised in tiny hand. Oneslipandit'sallover.

TCHING! The first blade landed a milli-inch above Fatima's left wrist.

TCHING! Another knife flew past her ear, even closer than the last.

A third knife was ready now, the one that would land above her head. . .

Bomp. Bomp. Bomp. She could feel her heart beating like a monkey's toy drum. The Wheel of Death began to spin. Faster and faster. . .

She trusted her brother like no other, but knew that a single mistake from him would mean the end of her short life.

"Cuthbert be calm, and steady be thine arm," her twin told himself. From behind his blindfold he could see nothing. Not the frightenedandpaleface of his sister, not the slack-jawed audience, not Macabre himself, preening his moustache and thinking dark thoughts.

Drumroll.

Daggerflash.

Applause!

CHAPTER TWO

In which a Storm Rages

ADMIT ONE

MACABRE'S
TRAVELLING CIRCUS
NOTE: PURCHASE OF THIS TICKET GUARANTEES NEITHER
THE SAFETY NOR THE ENTERTAINMENT OF THE SPECTATOR

The Big Top was now deserted, the handful of spectators long since returned home. Outside, the wind had turned into a storm, howling like a ghostly out-of-tune choir around the top of the great tent, whistling in and out of flapping canvas and between creaking tent-pegs. . . .

Macabre wasn't in a good mood. He rarely was. But tonight his mood was stormier than the night itself. He stood in the middle of the ring, whilst a single spotlight shone down on Cuthbert and Fatima, the Gruesome Twosome.

Macabre didn't speak at first, but continued to pace the sawdust, his top hat so toweringly tall it seemed almost lost in the upper reaches of the tent.

When finally he spoke his moustache quivered

with jealous rage "So, you wretched little brats. . ."

Cuthbert gripped Fatima's hand and gave it a reassuring squeeze.

"Another shabby display, full of missed moves and tame tricks!"

'That's not true! We're the best act you have!" protested Fatima, and she would have said more but Cuthbert nudged her hard. He knew she'd already said too much.

Macabre was bending down, so close that they could see the red veins in his eyes and the cracks in his thick white make-up. He shouted right into their faces.

"What delusion! If you're so good, then how come the Big Top was almost empty? I've seen more drama from Madame Mimi's Performing Poodles! More thrills from a troop of sleeping fleas! And after all the hours of training with which I've nurtured you!"

Cuthbert and Fatima bowed their heads meekly, not daring to answer back. They knew inside that theirs was the best act in the show. That when the Wheel of Death began to spin and the knives began to fly, every heart in the audience pitter-pattered with fear, how when they juggled with swords, the audience didn't dare look, how when Cuthbert's blindfold went on, even the most hard-hearted spectator couldn't help but cry out.

But Cuthbert and Fatima said nothing. They didn't dare.

FATIMA'S DIARY

We have always been in the circus. I can't remember anything else. Nothing about parents or candyfloss or bedtime stories. Nothing nice. Neither can Cuthbert and he's five minutes older than me.

We were performers even before we could walk. Macabre called us the "Bouncing Babes". He made us bounce up and down on a huge trampoline, and then he taught us how to do somersaults and flips. It was very frightening for us 'cos we were only a few months old. Then, one day, baby Cuthbert was performing an elaborate spin when he brought his dinner back up over the front row. It was then that we learned how to dodge knives, Macabre's knives. When he saw how agile we were, and how quick, he put us at the top of the bill and called us the "Gruesome Twosome".

Macabre made to grab Cuthbert by the neck, but the youngster was too quick, and instead the ringmaster snatched only thin air. This made him angrier still.

"Go and practise some more, you miserable little urchins! And don't show your faces again until you have attained PERFECTION!"

The Gruesome Twosome nodded. What else could they do?

Macabre strode off into the shadows, leaving Cuthbert and Fatima alone. Alone, as they'd always been. Outside they heard the wind blowing ever more fiercely.

"We have to escape!" whispered Cuthbert.

A tear started to wind its way down Fatima's cheek, but she stopped it with the back of her hand.

"We will," she muttered with steely determination, "we will."

CHAPTER THREE

Ten Years Earlier. . .

The lighthouse at Finefinger Point was constructed early in the seventeenth century by Eugene Vanburg, making it one of the county's oldest. It took more than thirty years to build and cost the lives of twelve men, most of whom were killed whilst laying kitchen-tiles during a hurricane.

R J SINGLETON, *A Lengthy Guide to Lighthouses of the Northern Peninsula.*

At Finefinger Point the fog never clears. It is there in the morning, wrapped around the rocks, it is there at midday, when the tide finally rolls out, and it is there in the evening when even the great beam from the lighthouse can scarcely cut through the briny gloom.

And there was fog in the life of Barrabas O'Hanlon too. He was the lighthouse keeper at Finefinger Point and had lived in that lonely spot all his life. His father had been the keeper of the light also, and *his* father before him. Barrabas had always imagined that one day his own children would take on the same title, and climb the nine hundred and eighty-five steps to the glass tower overlooking the cliffs. But Barrabas didn't have children. Not any more. Not since that day in 19– –, when the fog had descended on himself and his family. A cruel and impenetrable fog:

Babies snatched from local hospital!

TWINS TAKEN IN KIDDY-NAP HORROR!

Rattled! No clues in case of missing tots!

Mrs O'Hanlon had given birth to two fine sprogs. Twins. She had written to her husband with the happy news (being a lighthouse keeper he was of course unable to leave his post, not even for the birth of his own children), but how delighted he was to receive the news and to see the picture his wife had taken of the two babies. How tiny they were, how wrinkled like prunes! Cuthbert and Fatima: what fine names they had chosen!

The weeks passed and Barrabas eagerly scanned the horizon for the mail-boat that would bring him more news. One grey day, the sound of excited black-winged gulls had drawn him to the balcony. The black-winged gull was a species local to the area. On the day a large envelope arrived for the lighthouse keeper, a huge group of them gathered on the rocks below. He heard their shriek and squawk in the distance as he opened the envelope. How odd that it too was black.

Barrabas read without blinking. Mistswirl over his boots, crashofwaves inside his head.

Dear Mr Ohanlon,

We regret to inform you of the loss of your 2 children in a kiddnapping incident on the night of ——. Whilst we consider ourselves in no way responsible for the aforementioned incident, this being the work of a criminal(s) unknown, please rest assured we are doing everything in our power to recover the lost children (2).

Should the children be found we shall of course return them to you at your earliest convenience,
Yours regretfully,

N Fettock
Mrs N A Fettock,
Hospital Director,
Foghorn Falls.

Barrabas put down the letter and stood with his head bowed. The great light pulsed against his face every 7.8 seconds until even the gulls fell silent.

CHAPTER FOUR

Take down the Big Top!

*P*erformance over. Wind still howling. In their dressing room, Mr Spangly and his troupe of clowns crowd round the mirror but don't take off their make-up, (Macabre doesn't let them). The ringmaster himself, stalking the muddy showground, top hat reflecting in puddles, green teeth grinding, makes his way to Cuthbert and Fatima, still practising as instructed, and stands over them, allinblackshadow.

"We leave at dawn. Take down the Big Top and store the apparatus in carriages five to ten."

Cuthbert looked at his sister. A secret look, a hopeless look. How could they ever hope to take down the great tent in this storm? Two small tots, hundreds of metres of canvas, metal cable, ropes, and a raging storm?

"All part of your training, my dears," grinned Macabre, hoping for a word or two of protest. It never came, for the Gruesome Twosome had long since grown wise to Macabre's pleasure in their discomfort. They knew to accept their lot in silence and kept their true thoughts; their anger, their plans, hidden deep inside, to be shared only in moments alone.

There was not even a moon to guide them as their

tiny fingers battled to dismantle the Big Top, its
canvas flapping like the wings of a great white bird,
swan-white against the night. Clashofmetal, bolts
unscrewed.

"Throw down that trapeze!"

The other performers passed by in silence: the
Remarkable Otto, flexing his biceps and preening
his beard; Mr Spangly, chewing on a blade of damp
grass, eyes downcast; Olga the Bearded Lady, reading
the *Circus News*:

Days of the Big Top are numbered!

A special report by our entertainment correspondent.

"Why doth no one like us here?" Cuthbert had asked
one day. "Why doth no one talk to us?"

"Because we are not like them," replied his sister, in
a low whisper, knowing that on the Circus Train,
even the walls had ears.

"Why are we not like them?"

"We are not from the circus, bro, that is why. We
were brought here."

"But Macabre says. . ."

"I know what he says. But I also know what I feel
in my heart, dearest Cuthbert. Why else would we
always try to flee this place? This is not our home."

"So where?" mumbled her sad-eyed sibling.

Fatima shrugged her shoulders. "Somewhere out
there. Somewhere clown-free, beneath the stars,
beyond the woods. I only wish I knew. . ."

Fatima's whole body ached. Every task in the circus, it appeared, was theirs to do. Was it because they were the youngest? Or because Macabre hated them? Or for some other reason she hadn't yet worked out? If they'd had a father, would he have treated them like this?

"Hold fast the canvas, bro!"

Cuthbert, hidden now beneath the windwhipped canvas, found it hard to keep still; he had to keep shifting his feet as he wrestled with the ropes, and there was cold rain in his hair.

"We could fly," he thought. "We could hold on to this tent, run forward into the storm and up up and away!"

"Cuthbert!" shouted his sister from across the darkening field. "Hold her steady, I'm coming towards you." The canvas had to be folded like a bedsheet, except it was of course a thousand times larger. On to the train they also had to carry and store: two trapezes, five cages, eight ropes, twelve drums, one baton, one whip, seven advertising hoardings, two containers filled with sawdust, animal feed, one clown's car and assorted props, various dumb-bells and weights, twenty-six boxes of costumes, assorted musical instruments, cables, tent pegs, cash tin, temporary seating, chairs, one flag, and two false beards.

A small chink of dawn had already entered the sky as the Gruesome Twosome finished their task. Too exhausted to think of escape, they crept back to their beds and fell instantly asleep. They didn't even hear the whistle sound as the train left town.

CHAPTER FIVE

Barrabas Once More

FOGHORN TRUMPETER
MISSING TWINS SIGHTED AT FAMOUS BEAUTY SPOT!

Octagenarian mountaineer, Miss Violet Malpass, believes she may have glimpsed Foghorn's kidnapped babies whilst on an ascent of Mount Gronfeld (1,485 metres).

Speaking to our reporter, the locally-based rambler recalls seeing a pair of babies fitting the description of the Foghorn Two.

Ten years earlier, back at Finefinger Point, tragedy was still in the briny air. . .

Smell of seaweed. Grey mist. Breaking waves. Cry of gulls.

Barrabas O'Hanlon looked out from his lonely lighthouse with more bad news to bear. Another letter had arrived from the hospital, informing him this time that his wife of seven years had died as a result of "complications and confusion" following the birth and subsequent disappearance of their two babies .

Until this moment Barrabas had drawn comfort from the thought that Helga, his wife, would help track down their stolen offspring. She was a large and resourceful woman. But now even this hope had been extinguished. Now it was all down to him. It was he, Barrabas O'Hanlon, who must travel to the mainland and uncover the trail. He, Barrabas, who must turn detective. But how? A lighthouse keeper can never leave his post. The light must be tended every day. Lives depend on it.

With a heavy heart, Barrabas took out his finest cormorant-quill pen, and some paper carefully torn from his nautical diary. He began to compose a letter to the Admiralty's Lighthouse Division, requesting relief from his post "in order to look for my babies who have been snatched from me". He knew it would be some weeks before the letter could be sent, for the supply boat only called at Finefinger Point on the tenth day of every month and the next visit was still eighteen days hence.

Barrabas scanned the horizon with his telescope. Where could they be, those poor frightened children, and in whose hands? His blood ran cold at the very thought of all the villainy in the great world beyond his own beloved shoreline.

CHAPTER SIX

Circus Train

When Macabre's circus travelled between towns it was conveyed by train. But this was no ordinary locomotive.

The Carnival Train had been in the Macabre family for generations. Unlike most trains it didn't run only on tracks. Oh no, its great iron wheels could also carry it across fields, down roads, over snow and ice. Anywhere, in fact, its driver pleased to go.

Though it had once been thought of as pleasing to the eye, down the years this great steaming beast of a locomotive had grown more and more frightening in appearance. The front of the train was now painted with a faded but terrifying picture of a clown's face. Where the clown's eyes should have been, two piercing lights shone instead. Mounted on the roof of the engine was a large rusting funnel, belching forth a pall of dense black smoke. Behind the driver's cabin was a crazy array of rattling, battered, jangling carriages and trailers.

I ain't never seen no train like it. And I lived next door to the railroad since I wuz a child. Well that night I was just looking out cos I thought I hear sumpen, and there it was, steamin and smokin, great sparks lightin up the sky, I ain't never seen nuthin like it. And it weren't no ordinary train. No sir, cos it was comin down the front street, even though there ain't no tracks there. And behind the train itself, well I swear you could see all sorts of strange animals like lions and tigers and suchlike, and they's all a-screamin and a-growlin and makin all kindza noise. So I took me and hid right under my bed till I heard the train no more. . .

Each of the circus performers had their own compartment aboard the Carnival Train. Except for Macabre of course, who had a whole carriage to himself. The clowns slept next door, along with some noisy penguins; their compartment was filled with balloons and hooters, and tricks of every kind. Often at night, Macabre would have to bang the walls of his carriage to silence them.

The next carriage down contained the witch, Badhagg, and a couple of Madame Mimi's performing poodles. Then came the fire-eater, Fire-and-Brimstone, who shared with Olga the Bearded Lady. The wild animals had an open-topped carriage to themselves. At night you could hear them roar and snarl and grind their teeth.

Cuthbert and Fatima occupied the very end compartment of the very end carriage. It was positioned directly above the rear axle, so that whenever the train hit a bump everything in the compartment would rattle and shake, candles would blow out, pictures smash to the ground. But they still preferred it to any of the other compartments because it was the furthest away from Macabre. It was home, if you could ever call a train compartment home.

And now the Carnival Train was steaming away from Dosgtooth as fast as the clowns could shovel coal into her boiler.

Macabre sat slumped in his favourite chair, the one made from chimpanzee skin, counting the night's takings, "One . . . two . . . three . . . four . . . five. . . Five pennywigs!"

The frowning ringmaster emptied the coins out of his upturned top hat and flung them across the room to where he had summoned his closest advisers: the witch, Badhagg, Mr Spangly the clown, and a gaggle of fierce-looking penguins.

Badhagg looked up from her crystal ball. "You're in a bad mood tonight," she cackled, with a voice as dry as autumn leaves. She picked up the coins and shoved them down one of her stockings.

"*You'd* be in a bad mood if you saw how much money this circus was losing," snarled Macabre. "I'd be better off selling the lot."

"Perhaps you should?" replied Badhagg. "There isn't any call for circuses these days. All the kids want is poppsycorn and movies and—"

"—AND THE CIRCUS!" Macabre's moustache twirled as he snarled. "Kids love circuses. They always have and they always will. Even if I have to make them!"

The train was speeding through a foggy, frostbound landscape not stopping for anyone or anything. It flew through red signals and across level crossings, woe betide anything which crossed its tracks!

Two fierce penguins waddled into the compartment, bearing Macabre's hot-water bottle, made from finest polar bear fur.

"I'm too kind, too easy going," grumbled Macabre, using the steam from the hot-water bottle to curl his moustache. "That's my trouble. If I look at that performance tonight, what do I see? The clowns weren't funny. Madame Mimi's poodles made us a laughing stock. Our strong man couldn't punch a hole in a paper bag. As usual the only ones the audience liked were those knife-throwing, show-stealing freaks, the Gruesome Twosome! Heaven help us if they ever succeeded in escaping!"

"They won't," said Mr Spangly. "We keep them under lock and key. We won't let you down."

Macabre wasn't placated by the clown's words.

He rose to his feet, still clutching the hot-water bottle, and yelled across the carriage, "From now on we rise at five a.m. and practise until dark. And we'll keep doing it until you buffoons get things right. Right?!"

Macabre glanced around the room and found no signs of disagreement. Mr Spangly crossed his giant feet and looked down at the floor. Badhagg stared into her crystal ball and bit her lip. The penguins said nothing. But in the very end compartment of the very end carriage, far from view, a mutiny was brewing.

CHAPTER SEVEN

Warpaint!

Cuthbert and Fatima never gave up on their dream of escape. Which is why, once they'd recovered from their exertions taking down the Big Top, the old spirit soon returned. Now they sat whispering in their compartment, dressed in Red Indian costume, carrying bows and arrows, full of impossible hopes.

"Saddle the mustangs!" cried Cuthbert. "Prepare the warpaint!"

Cuthbert and Fatima began to paint their faces, using make-up borrowed from Olga the Bearded Lady, until their disguise was complete and they resembled nothing less than genuine bona fide Native Americans.

Fatima took a bow from her quiver and a piece of rope. She tied one end to a bar on the window and the other to the arrow. Then she took hold of her bow, gripping it expertly between small, bony fingers.

This wasn't the first time that Cuthbert and Fatima had tried to escape. No. They'd tried many times before. . . Once, during a performance, Fatima had aimed the Strongman's cannon up towards the roof of the Big Top, and fired her brother to freedom. Only she'd used too much gunpowder and he'd ended up in

Macabre's dressing room, black as soot, and trembling all over.

Then they had tried disguise: not easy when you're only four feet tall. Fatima balanced herself on Cuthbert's shoulders, and they dressed themselves as a bearded old man. They teetered towards the exit from the showground, and Fatima had felt sure they would make it – until a chance sneeze by Cuthbert ruined the disguise and gave the game away, right in front of Macabre and his clown henchmen.

Each time they were captured, the ringmaster made their lives even more difficult. They'd be starved for a day. Kept in chains for a week. Forced to clean out the elephant's quarters all winter. . .

The Carnival Train continued to rattle on, through frozen fields and sleepy hamlets, past deserted signal boxes and icy lakes.

"Will this work?" whispered Cuthbert. "Our plans never do. . ."

Fatima shrugged her frail shoulders. "I can't promise, dear bro, I don't know, but we have to keep trying, don't we?"

Cuthbert nodded but there was nothing but fear in his dark eyes. Fatima suddenly hesitated, wondering if their dreams of freedom were worth all this.

Cuthbert saw the doubt cross her face and took an arrow from his pouch and kissed it. "May your aim be true."

Fatima took up her bow and aimed at the largest tree she could see. The arrow flew whistlefast and straight, landing with a satisfying CLUNG!, right in the middle of a broadleaved oak. Within seconds the rope tightened, ripping the bars free. Icy wind whistled all around their compartment.

"Is this freedom?" asked Cuthbert, who'd never felt it before.

Fatima didn't answer. She grabbed her brother's hand and led him to the hole where the bars of the window used to be. Since they'd been on rations of bread and water all autumn, there was just enough room for the two of them to squeeze through. The only trouble was that the Carnival Train was still racing along at great speed.

Tchacketychack, tchacketychack. . .

Fatima threw their bags clear of the train. Then their pogo-sticks. No going back now.

Cuthbert began to tremble. "Must we leap down there?"

"Yes, don't be frightened. I'm with you. Take my hand."

The wind blew in their faces. The stars were swimming all around, everything dizzy as a fairground ride as Cuthbert and Fatima leapt from the speeding train and into the great unknown.

At the very same moment, a large black balloon in Macabre's room suddenly burst, waking him so violently he almost fell from his chair. Not realizing what it portended, the evil ringmaster fell back into a deep sleep and didn't wake until the following morning. . .

CHAPTER EIGHT

The Legendary Patience of the Lighthouse Keeper

Barrabas O'Hanlon looked much older than he really was. "Weather-beaten" might be the word: a face shaped by the wind and storms that lashed the cliffs o'er which the great white lighthouse perched. And aged too, by the many months and years he had waited for a ship to bring another keeper to relieve him, or for the police to bring news of his lost children. At first the case had attracted a lot of attention, but little by little, the police lost interest in the whole affair. They had other crimes to consider: a missing set of ladders in Dogstooth, a phantom balloon popper in Darkwood. In addition, they told him, sightings were getting thin on the ground and they were short of personnel. It eventually reached the stage where they scarcely ever wrote to Barrabas at all.

How many years had it been since he had first communicated to the authorities his request for leave to search for his kidnapped babies? It had been many years, but even those years seemed longer, for time travels exceedingly slow when one is alone on a lighthouse. Especially Finefinger Point, where each day is like the one before, for there are no seasons to be seen, the fog never rising from the shore.

Not that Barrabas had wasted the time. When not engaged in his lighthouse duties (cleaning and checking the lamp, looking out for shipwrecks, writing in his logbook) he read every book he could find on the subject of detectives and their work. If the police were unable to locate his vanished off-spring, then maybe he could. Fortunately his late wife had possessed quite a collection of crime novels. If he, a humble lighthouse keeper, were ever to find his long-lost brood, then he must know how to conduct an enquiry: where to search, who to ask. Motive. Evidence. *Modus operandi.* These were all new terms to Barrabas at first, but slowly and surely he acquainted himself with his future profession.

But when would he ever be able to leave the lighthouse? Ships came and ships went, but no word ever reached him from the Admiralty's Lighthouse Division.

Each time the supply ship arrived, Barrabas would rush down the nine hundred and eighty-five stone steps – how clean he kept those steps – and greet the sailors in their brightly painted boat, bobbing up and down in the seaweed and spray. Eagerly he would reach for the picture of Cuthbert and Fatima, his lost babies, and enquire, "Have you, in your travels, ever come across two tiny tots who look like this? Except they will by now be ten years older. . ."

Shakes of bearded heads. Blank faces. No one had ever seen anything. Not a shred of evidence in all that time.

But Barrabas O'Hanlon was a patient man, as lighthouse keepers often are, and one day, that patience would surely be rewarded. . .

The rowing boat emerged out of the gloom without the lighthouse keeper having even known it was there. The first he knew of her presence was a single horn sounding, then the crunch of boots on shingle and wetsand.

"My name is Atkins," said a stranger with a kitbag over his shoulder and long black sideburns. "The Admiralty have sent me to take over from you. I apologize for the delay in coming but we were delayed by bad weather."

"For ten years?"

"Yes. Most unfortunate."

Barrabas stood motionless. In the relentless strobing of the beacon, Atkins's form changed from lightness to dark every 7.8 seconds. Then, as if woken from a dream, Barrabas grasped his fellow keeper by the hand and shook it warmly. "Come inside my good fellow, there's tea on the stove. My bags are already packed, I must try to catch the return tide tonight."

In his heart Barrabas was already on the mainland, striding the cobbled streets, picture in hand.

"Have you, by any chance, ever come across two tiny tots who look like this? Except by now they will be ten years older. . ."

CHAPTER NINE

In which Macabre Receives a Pressing Invitation

No one at the circus ever got much mail. That was mainly on account of Macabre. "Bad news comes in envelopes", he was fond of saying, and for that reason gave orders to his clown guards that postmen were not welcome within sight of the Big Top.

So it was a surprise to all, that dark and frosty morn, when Mr Spangly appeared in Macabre's compartment, clutching a large golden envelope.

Mr Spangly wasn't the wisest of clowns – and clowns are not wise in the first place – but he knew to tread carefully on this occasion. He carried the envelope as though it were a bundle of high explosives, and already his eyes glistened with tears. He coughed to announce his presence.

"Ahem!"

Macabre looked up, then looked down again, and continued writing in a large red ledger.

"I hope that's not what I think it is, Mr Spangly, or you may be swinging upside down from the trapeze tonight."

Mr Spangly thrust the letter towards his master as though it were burning his fingers.

"I had to take it. They said you would cover me with gold when you read it. Or something like that. They, they, er, said you would be p-pleased with me."

"Ah, but I'm not pleased, Mr Spangly."

This unexpectedly negative reaction threw the tearful clown off balance. His mouth opened and closed, but no words came out. He offered the envelope again.

Something about the gleaming gold envelope caught Macabre's attention. Against his better judgement he looked up from his accounts, put down his pen, and snatched the envelope from Mr Spangly's trembling hand.

"This had better be good!"

With long bony fingers, he sliced through the envelope and pulled out a letter. The letter was written in a long flowing hand on impressive handmade paper.

Mr Spangly's heart pitter-pattered with anxiety. If this letter turned out to be a bill or complaint then the clown knew he was as good as dead.

The Great Macabre's blood-red pupils narrowed as he began to read.

"Great and noble master of the Circus

(a fine beginning, he thought)

"At the request of His Royal Highness, the Maharajah of Rhajibangaloor, we do

hereby request the presence of the Great Finian Macabre and his travelling Circus Troupe for the purposes of performance and entertainment. . ."

The ringmaster's white make-up cracked in a nearlysmile. He liked what he was reading.

"In consideration of the sum of 100,000 rupees, we summon the aforementioned to give one week of performances at the Palace of Bahg-aloo.

We shall expect your attendance on the ——— of the ———— at 19.00 hours.

"One hundred thousand rupees!" The Great Macabre leapt to his feet, on the point of embracing Mr Spangly. The moment passed without him doing so, but there was no doubting his delight at the contents of the letter. He continued reading:

"All arrangements for your travel have been made. The Maharajah's ship, The Eastern Star, will convey you to Rhajibangaloor. She sets sail from the Foghorn Shiphorn Co. terminal at 00.45 hrs on the —th. Please

be there, at the exact hour stipulated, or this contract will be void."

Macabre glanced at the calendar on his wall, which was four years old, then recalculated the actual date in his mind.

"That's the morning after Halloween! We must be at the terminal by the end of the week!"

Mr Spangly didn't quite understand all this talk of terminals and shipping companies.

"But we always take the train," he mumbled.

Macabre was staring out of the shutters at the dawn sky, dreaming of a brighter future. "Plenty of room for our train on the Maharajah's boat. We will travel in style, Mr Spangly."

Mr Spangly picked up the letter that had so revived his fortunes.

"There is a PS—"

Macabre grabbed the letter and scanned quickly to the bottom of the page. "At the request . . . bla-bla . . . in consideration of . . . bla-bla . . . I remain, sir, your obedient servant, Srikkanth Malhottra, secretary to His most excellent Highness, the Maharajah of Rhajibangaloor.

"PS The Maharajah has especially requested that he meet in person that incredible and most death-defying duo, the "Gruesome Twosome" as he has heard

*excellent reports of their performances.
Please ensure that they are given "top
billing" on the show and are able to meet
with his exaltedness backstage."*

Mr Spangly's heart-rate accelerated like a runaway dodgem. He knew the letter was suddenly not such good news. Macabre's expression changed in an instant, and the clown instinctively took two paces back.

"The Gruesome Twosome! Why does he want to see THEM? A cheap two-a-penny knife-throwing act!"

"Because they're goo—" began Mr Spangly, who had not yet learned there are some questions it is better to leave unanswered.

"They're *what*?" snapped Macabre, green teeth flashing in the candlelight.

"N-n-nothing," stuttered the clown, realizing his error just in time.

Macabre began pacing the floor, still holding the letter in his hand.

"No matter. This letter changes everything!" he hissed in triumph. "Thus is the future of Macabre's Circus assured. Farewell Foghorn Falls! Farewell dismal Dogstooth! A brighter future awaits Finian Macabre." And his laugh echoed into the air, mingling with the sound of pistons and steel and grinding metal.

CHAPTER TEN

The Alarm is Raised

A silver-hatted clown rushed from carriage to carriage, raising the alarm.

"Oh dear, oh calamity!" he muttered to himself on seeing the Gruesome Twosome's empty compartment. And when he spotted the missing bar on the window and felt the wind rushing against his white-painted face, he knew there was trouble in store. Terrible trouble!

All along the Carnival Train, news spread of Cuthbert and Fatima's escape. Luggage trunks were opened, sheets unravelled, bunks emptied. Sinister clowns poked their painted faces into every conceivable nook and cranny.

Macabre opened his mouth and roared.

"Gone! How can they be gone?" screamed the ringmaster on being told the news. "We didn't make a single stop last night! Search the train! Search everywhere!"

And Macabre also wasted no time in summoning the evil witch, Badhagg to his carriage. She wasn't used to rising so early in the day and arrived in a bad mood.

"You know I don't like to work while the train's travelling," she sniffed. "It causes problems with the receiver on my crystal ball."

Macabre grabbed hold of the witch's bony shoulders and hoisted her off the ground. "The Maharajah of Rhajibangaloor has demanded to see them and see them he must! The future of the circus depends upon it!"

He span the witch around like some very frightening voodoo doll. Mr Spangly was forced to take evasive action.

"You'd better find those two runaways, Badhagg, or I'll feed you to the lions!"

Badhagg blew her nose and muttered to herself. She didn't care to be spoken to like that but knew Macabre's threats were not idle. She was in his power and had been for many years. . .

Long ago and far away, Macabre and his circus had once performed this same tawdry travelling show. But in those days the Big Top was more full than empty, the band a little more in tune, the lions younger and with a full set of teeth each.

One autumn eve – a fine night with a sky dusted with stars – the witch Badhagg was at work in the ring, reading fortunes and gazing into her crystal ball.

It was a popular part of the act, and the black-clad crone almost enjoyed her moment in the spotlight (if not the spotlight itself, which hurt her eyes and showed unkindly the blemishes on her warty skin).

"I see a tall, dark stranger in your life," she intoned dramatically to a lady in the front row.

"That'll be my husband," exclaimed the lady, clasping her hands delightedly. "He's five foot seven and seldom home!"

A murmur of delight and surprise rang around the Big Top. Macabre preened his moustache as he always did when things were going well.

"I see a flight across night skies," continued Badhagg, with goggle eyes and a wicked grin.

The lady in the front row looked at her companion and her brow furrowed. "I, I . . . don't like to fly," she stammered.

"Not you, me!" hissed the witch. "It's Halloween and I got people to see!"

"But what about my reading?" spluttered the lady. "What happens to me? Will I get a new hat for the autumn fair?"

Badhagg fixed the luckless spectator with a cold-eyed stare that ended any protest before it could begin. But the watching Macabre was not so easily pacified.

"Stay where you are, witch!" he snarled, and the audience took in a sharp breath. Was this all part of the act, they wondered? It was a bit frightening if it was. Jaws dropped open with popcorn poised in plump white palms as Badhagg confronted Macabre, resplendent in his black top hat and cloak.

"In case you haven't heard," snapped the witch, angrily, "it's Halloween and NOBODY tells a witch what to do on Halloween!"

If Macabre was taken aback he didn't show it. Instead he began to finger the bolt of the lion cage beside which he was standing.

Badhagg paused for a moment, surprised perhaps her exit from the ring was to go unchallenged. She turned to the audience.

"Thank you, ladies and gentlemen, and goodnight. Apologies that the show was a little on the short side tonight." There were one or two angry whistles. Macabre let slide the bolt. The audience gasped. With a loud roar, the largest of the two circus lions rushed forwards into the ring, heading straight for Badhagg.

"Ooooh!" The crowd's reaction alerted the witch to the fact that something was wrong, and she spun around. Badhagg fumbled for a spell but there was no time. The lion stood before her. A golden mane. Black snout. Hot breath. Bared teeth. Pink tonsils.

"Aaaargh!" The terrified witch suddenly found herself examining the lion's throat at close quarters, her hands jamming open its jaws, feet kicking and struggling on the sawdust as all around the crowd gasped and squealed.

"Help!" Her cry was muffled inside the lion's mouth. "Help me!"

The Great Macabre stroked his moustache, examined a fingernail and enjoyed the fear and tension in the crowd. Then slowly, whip in hand, he began to cross the ring.

Lion and witch were still engaged in a battle of

strength, with the odds seemingly in favour of the former.

"Didn't see THIS in your crystal ball, did you?" hissed Macabre, just loud enough so that the crowd could hear.

"He-elp!" groaned the witch, her arms growing more tired by the second. "Get him off me!"

Macabre's shadow fell over the lion and the witch.

"What would it be worth?"

No answer came from within the lion's jaws. The crowd pressed forward, mouths open, plump children neverseenawitchgeteat before. Badhagg felt the lion's jaw closing tighter and tighter.

"Anything . . . gold . . . silver . . . brass. . . Just get me out," she gasped.

Macabre was in no hurry. He glanced at the crowd, who still appeared to be enjoying the show, and then leaned forward, close enough to hear the lion's heavy breathing.

"You will be bound to me for twenty years," he barked at Badhagg. "I know my rights. Anyone who saves the life of a witch is entitled to twenty years of unquestioning service."

From the lion's jaw there came a loud crunch and Macabre feared for a moment he might have delayed too long.

"All right!" Badhagg replied hastily. "Anything. Now please . . . help. . ."

"Twenty years," repeated Macabre. "You agree to be bound to me for twenty years? To do as I command?

No Halloween flights? No fits of temper or bad tempered cackle? You serve me and only me?"

Silence.

"Yesss. All right. . ."

The deal was done.

Macabre's whip flashed across the ring, and his red eyes flashed in triumph. "A wise decision! . . .Ladies and gentlemen, I hope you have enjoyed tonight's show. Anyone not smiling as they leave will have cause to regret it."

He cracked his whip overhead and the lion released its grip on Badhagg and scampered back to its cage like a frightened kitten.

That night Badhagg did not fly across halloween skies with the other witches, but spent time in Macabre's carriage, putting her signature to a bond of twenty years' service. Her heart was heavy and the hatred in it burned as hot as fire.

Back on the Carnival Train, Macabre opened his mouth and roared again, "Find them!"

"Very well then," wheezed the witch. "No need to get your top hat in a twist." Badhagg hunched over her crystal ball and watched patiently until it began to glow. Soon an eerie light filled the whole compartment.

"Interesting!" Badhagg drew closer to the ball. "Mmmm . . . VERY interesting—"

Macabre could scarcely contain himself. "What! What is it?"

The witch looked up and winked. "A special offer on brooms at the local hardware store."

The giant ringmaster's face changed from red to purple. "This is no time for japes and jokes. Where are those kids, you stupid witch! Where are they?"

CHAPTER ELEVEN

Dry Land Greets Barrabas

THE DARKWOOD GAZETTE

Six months to the day since the disappearance of the famous Foghorn Falls Babies, police have reported a new lead in the investigation. Talking to a parent-toddler evening, Inspector Claude LeBlanc revealed that a child's rattle found in the woods near the Foghorn Maternity Hospital has provided valuable forensical evidence. Trained dogs are now combing the area and new developments are expected at any time.

Foghorn Falls loomed ahead, its whitewashed houses clinging to the shoreline like seabird eggs. It had been twelve years and thirty days since Barrabas O'Hanlon, lighthouse keeper, had last set foot on dry land. Twelve years and thirty days since he'd been somewhere the wind didn't howl all day filled with a salty spray, and where you couldn't see more than a stone's throw in front of your face on account of the fog.

Of course, he missed the wind and the rain and the cold seeping through his bones. And how out of place he felt, walking through the town with a bag in one hand and a picture of Cuthbert and Fatima clutched in the other. He sensed that people looked curiously at his lighthouse keeper's uniform: the peaked cap and high necked sweater, the wellington boots and the telescope. He was like a fish out of water. Like one of the crabs he'd so often seen stranded in the rock pools at the foot of the lighthouse. He longed to hurry back to the harbour and take a boat back to his beloved Finefinger Point. What would be happening there now? What great ships were being guided past deadly rocks by the brilliant beacon of *his* lighthouse? But then he remembered his quest and his own precious cargo of infants so painfully lost. He turned towards an old woman who had just emerged from the hardware store and paused for a moment to fasten her bonnet against the breeze.

"Excuse me, madam," began Barrabas, nervously, "have you, in your travels, ever come across two tiny tots who look like this? Except they will by now be ten years older. . ."

If Barrabas hoped his search would be easier on dry land, then he was soon disappointed. Like the detectives he had read so much about, he eagerly interviewed likely witnesses, many hundreds of them. But the trail seemed cold. It wasn't long before he began to understand why the police had terminated their interest in the case.

After yet another unsuccessful enquiry, the weary lighthouse keeper resolved to change tack and try instead to locate the hospital itself; the very spot where all those years ago his two babies had been

47

cruelly snatched. "The Crime Scene" as he now liked to call it.

This new plan pleased him and, after asking directions from a small boy on a tricycle, he marched quickly down the street in the direction of The Foghorn Falls Maternity Hospital, Whalemouth Drive.

CHAPTER TWELVE

Cuthbert and Fatima and their Pogo-sticks

As black night and the Carnival Train faded into the distance, Cuthbert and Fatima dusted themselves down. In their brief careers as the Bouncing Babes they'd soon learned how to fall great distances without hurting themselves.

"Which way?" asked Fatima when she'd got her breath back.

"It matters not, methinks," replied Cuthbert, picking up their impossibly large bags which also contained the two pogo-sticks on which they planned to make their escape.

In truth the Gruesome Twosome hadn't thought out this part of their plan at all. Deep down they imagined that somewhere along the line it would fail, as their plans usually did. Now it had succeeded, they had to decide where to flee. North, south, east, or west? Or some other direction?

Cuthbert was a shy and quiet boy, whose only hobby was reading books on Shakespeare and Ancient History. But he did remember one place where he and his sister had found happiness, if only for a few, fleeting moments.

"Recall, if you will, that old lady with whom we once spoke?"

Fatima smiled for the first time that month. "Mrs Hubbard?"

"The very same!"

And Cuthbert and Fatima's minds went back to a summer's day, not so very long ago, when they had met Mrs Amelia Hubbard for the first, and indeed, only time. . . .

Sometimes, when they were visiting a large town, Macabre would parade the whole circus down the main street. It was a sort of free preview for the locals. These were magical moments for the Gruesome Twosome, because, even though Macabre never let any of the performers out of his sight, it still meant a few precious hours away from the Big Top.

But on this one day, Cuthbert and Fatima had accidentally taken a wrong turn away from the rest of the parade, and found themselves in a strange backstreet halfway between an old graveyard and a row of large, ramshackle houses. At first they'd been frightened, but then they smelt apple pie and rose blossom. A shaft of watery sunlight shone down from the warm blue sky, and an elderly voice called out to them from over a hedge:

"I say, children! Would you care for some milk and cookies?"

Cuthbert and Fatima looked at each other and prepared to run. But something about the voice was so friendly it tempted them into staying. And when they looked up, with their shy little faces, they saw

Mrs Amelia Hubbard standing before them, elderly widow and sole resident of 22a Gravestone Walk, Windflower. Or at least that's what it said in the faded letters on her mailbox.

"I wondered if you might care for a little refreshment on this hot and stifling day?"

Cuthbert reached out a small, thin hand. He'd never seen a cookie before.

"And you too, my dear. . ."

Fatima sipped a glass of milk, so cool and refreshing.

"What strange little bodies you are. Where do you come from, my dears?"

But before Fatima could answer, the two children vanished suddenly from the old lady's view.

"What in tootin' tarnation!" gasped Mrs Hubbard, who'd never seen children disappear into thin air before. In their place there now stood another figure, dark in aspect and sulphurous in smell. He was tall, with bloodshot eyes and a black moustache. He preened his top hat with long, white, bloodless fingers. It was of course the Great Macabre.

He bowed down before the elderly widow with an elaborate flourish. In taking off his top hat it seemed that somehow Cuthbert and Fatima had vanished inside, for when he replaced it again, there was no sign of the two children. "It may be the only trick I know, but it's a good one," Macabre hissed to himself, before turning his attentions back to the frail old lady standing before him.

"Good day, Madame." The ringmaster smiled at old

Mrs Hubbard, with sharkjagged teeth. "Allow me to present you with this free complimentary ticket to last night's show."

"Why, thank you. But where are the children? They haven't finished their milk and cookies."

Macabre was already striding off down the street. "They must practise practise practise! Thank you for looking after them for me!"

His teeth were gritted and he ground them all the way back to the main street. "You will suffer for this, urchins! Milk and cookies are not good for little children!"

Fatima snapped out of her daydream. A fine rain was now drip-dripping off the end of her pogo-stick.

"You are right, Cuthbert. It is to Mrs Hubbard that we must go!"

And so, loading their impossibly large bags on to their shoulders, they bounced off in the direction of Windflower.

"Are you sure this is the way?" asked Fatima after a mile or two.

"Oh yes," replied Cuthbert. "I feel it in my bones."

"I think that might be the concrete road."

But Cuthbert was right. Windflower did indeed lie in that direction. The smell of the sea and the memory of a kind act continued to draw them on like a beacon, shining through the autumnal gloom. Like a lighthouse one might almost say. . .

CHAPTER THIRTEEN

Crime Scene

The last babies to be born at The Foghorn Falls Maternity Hospital had wailed their little lungs out nine years earlier. Now it was Barrabas walking through the empty, echoing corridor, trying to imagine how different things would have been when his late wife, Helga, had first arrived there: full of hope and excitement, chatting to the nurses in her strange accent, missing the wind and rain of her lighthouse home.

Barrabas was surprised at how small the hospital was. Just five small rooms, empty now of course, and an office at the end of the corridor. A door blew open and shut in the distance. It was late afternoon and the light was already beginning to fade as Barrabas made his tour of the building. He took fingerprints, paced creaking floors, wrote in his notebook, and searched for clues.

But several hours later not a trace had been found of his lost babies.

"So much for the great detective!" he thought angrily. "Here I am, at the scene of the crime, walking in the very footsteps of the kidnappers themselves, but where are the clues?" He remembered another word, "forensic", which detectives often used but there was no sign of that either. No sign of anything in this old hospital now but dust. He chided himself for his foolish expectations. What had he really expected to find? A note from the kidnappers? A map leading him to their secret lair?

The door at the end of the corridor was still blowing open and shut. The noise irritated the lighthouse keeper, who was used to silence. But when he tried to close the door, he saw that the lock was broken. As he looked more closely, Barrabas noticed the piece of paper that had been used to wedge the door open was now zigzagging down the corridor.

"Forensic," he muttered to himself. "It might be forensic. A good detective leaves no stone unturned."

Barrabas picked up the scrap of paper, covered in dust, blew it, and read, slowly. It didn't make much sense for he only had half of the original.

BE THE...
YOUR FORTUNE
CANDYFLOSS
TOFFEE APPLES
ICE COLD DRINKS

PERFORMANCE BEGINS 19.30
LATECOMERS WILL BE PUNISHED

Barrabas looked around to see if there was more. But though he combed the whole building for a second time he could find nothing that linked to his only clue, just dead moths and dust.

He looked at the writing again. It was very large. It must have been printed, he guessed.

YOUR FORTUNE

It seemed as though fortune was both smiling and taunting him at the same time. What a coincidence it would have to be if this fragment of paper were to have anything at all to do with his missing babes. And yet. . .

CANDYFLOSS
TOFFEE APPLES
ICE COLD DRINKS

Barrabas didn't know much about babies, even though he had once been one, but it seemed to him that candyfloss, toffee apples and ice cold drinks were not things that babies would normally consume.

PERFORMANCE BEGINS 19.30

7.30 p.m.? Babies were generally in bed by then. Or could this be some entertainer come to entertain the newborn babes and their proud mothers? And perhaps whilst at the hospital this kindly entertainer saw his own Cuthbert and Fatima? For the first time in many a storm-lashed day, hope stole into the lighthouse keeper's heart.

"I will find this entertainer and he will have news of my babies. How they looked. How they gurgled. He alone will remember them as they were!"

Barrabas scurried from the hospital, clutching the precious fragment of paper in his hand. He knew what any detective would know: find the printer who printed this sheet and you find the entertainer: the kindly fellow with the toffee apples and candyfloss who made the children laugh and smile. . .

CHAPTER FOURTEEN

THE GREED GAZETTE
DENTIST FLEES LION

Dentist Miss Olivia Tuckle (25), was yesterday forced to flee for her life when an African lion (8), believed to be from a local circus, entered her surgery at 10, Rillington Place. Local police later made a thorough search of the area but could find no trace of the beast. The public have been asked to shoot the creature on sight.

*B*adhagg and Macabre stood at the front of the train as it rumbled through a wooded valley. The witch had long since lost the signal on her crystal ball.

"You realize that without those two brats the circus is finished?" growled the ringmaster, holding on to his hat to stop it from being blown off. "It would take me years to train another act that good . . . we could never fool the Maharajah and bang goes our hundred thousand rupees."

Badhagg grinned. "We'll find them. Don't we always find the runaways? They won't get far . . . not using pogo-sticks."

Macabre nodded, reassured, and thought back to the night, ten or so years ago, when first he'd clapped eyes on Cuthbert and Fatima. . .

Foghorn Falls Maternity Hospital, one snowy Christmas Eve. Macabre remembered how he and Mr Spangly had slowly slid open a window and crept inside.

Snowonboots, handsofice.

"Ssschhhhh!"

As their eyes grew accustomed to the gloom, they saw row upon row of sleeping babies.

"Perfect!" hissed Macabre to his red-nosed accomplice in crime. "Get them young – that's the key to finding a great circus act. Get them young and train them hard!"

Mr Spangly felt like crying at the sight of all those tiny innocent babies gurgling peacefully in their sleep.

"What about these two?" Macabre whispered from across the hospital ward, and held aloft two small babies. "They seem nicely balanced. . ."

Macabre threw the babies to Mr Spangly who had to leap nimbly in order to catch them. They certainly felt nice and light.

"Do you have the sack?" hissed Macabre.

Mr Spangly nodded obediently.

The sudden shrill shrieking of the Carnival Train's whistle interrupted Macabre's memories. . .

"Easy to lose them in this countryside," he growled, as more trees flashed by in the twilight. "Too many woods. Once we reach that clearing I want you to try the crystal ball again."

Badhagg nodded.

The wheels of the Carnival Train span faster and faster and great clouds of black smoke blew out from under them. Clowns shovelled coal into her fires and the days of the Gruesome Twosome were surely numbered. . .

CHAPTER FIFTEEN

By Pogo-stick . . .

*E*ven the feel of a chill autumn wind in their hair thrilled the Gruesome Twosome. And more wonderful still was the sight of the great canopy of stars twinkling overhead as they lay down to sleep.

"I never dreamed it would be like this to be free," said Fatima as she made a bed among the twigs and leaves of a dark forest.

"I did," answered Cuthbert. "Every single night."

For hour after hour their pogo-sticks had carried them through the ever-changing autumnal landscape. Along dank, muddy tracks, past sleepy, ramshackle farmsteads, through dark, forbidding woods and spinneys, frosted and windblown and occasionally lashed by rain.

With each bounce of their pogo-sticks they drew both closer to Windflower and further from the reach of the Great Macabre. Or so they thought. They had no way of knowing if either impression were true.

"Is he still on our trail, do you think?" whispered Cuthbert in the wooded gloom.

"Indubitably," replied his sister. "He needs us. We're top of the bill. Without us the circus will close."

"That's sad."

"Don't feel sorry for them, Cuthbert. They don't care for us. If Macabre were ever to take us back there –" Fatima stopped mid-sentence. She didn't want to frighten Cuthbert. An owl hooted from across the wood and the moon glanced out like a shiningsilverlantern. "Now go to sleep, for we've still many miles to travel."

FATIMA'S DIARY

The search for Windflower...

DAY ONE
No sign of Macabre or the Circus Train. We have travelled all day following Cuthbert's instincts.

DAY TWO
Passed through a small town. Saw circus posters advertising our show. Our hearts sank. Spent the night in an old barn with rats and racoons and feeling the ringmaster would stride in and snatch us back at any time.

DAY THREE
It rained all day and Cuthbert caught a cold. Frightened his sneezing might give us away.

DAY FOUR
Cold and tired. We were glad to find a field of pumpkins. Not all had been harvested for Halloween . . . our first

meal in a long time. The night was clear and starlit but so very cold.

DAY FIVE
Cuthbert says we are near to the sea. Certainly the wind has grown stronger. The sight of a distant train made our hearts skip a beat but it was just an old locomotive carrying wheat and hobos.

DAY SIX
Passed through a town called Rooksville. It seemed deserted, but there were many Halloween decorations. We have almost lost track of the days now, but we are sure it is Halloween tomorrow. Why does that fact fill us with a certain dread?
There has been no sign of Macabre or the carnival train so we should think ourselves once more safe, but actually each day the sense of dread seems greater.

HALLOWEEN
The night when witches fly and evil things roam. We must be VERY careful. . .

CHAPTER SIXTEEN

By Train . . .

The old farmer rubbed his eyes, then placed his wrinkled hands back on the pitchfork, holding it raised against the approaching danger. Billowing black smoke filled the air along with the mechanical grind of iron on steel.

At the last possible moment, seeing that the train was not about to stop, the elderly man was forced to throw himself to one side. He watched in amazement as the Carnival Train thundered past, all sparks and steam and lions' roar.

"Out of the way!" shouted Mr Spangly from the footman's plate, whilst inside his luxuriously appointed compartment, the Great Macabre stared at the tattered map spread out before him. The map was some years out of date and, in truth, Macabre couldn't read maps. The various names and places swam before his bloodshot eyes.

"Which way will they run? Which way will they turn?"

None of his penguin lieutenants dared make a reply. Wrong answers in Macabre's company were ruthlessly punished. Interested silence was always a much safer option.

As day followed dreary day, Macabre and his crew

63

were unceasing in their search for the escaped children. This train followed no timetable and didn't stop for any signals. When the tracks ahead were rusted or broken, it left them and thundered on across fields or down roads.

Dayandnight, dayandnight, dayandnight. Macabre's eyes were sleepless orbs with dark rings like shadow; there was no time to eat or sleep. The Maharajah's invitation was never far from his thoughts, nor the fast approaching deadline when the boat would set sail for the fabulous East.

"Why did they leave?" he snarled one night, as the candles burned low. "This was their home. I gave them everything. A place in the show. . ."

A pause while the crew tried to think of something else Macabre had given them.

"Nice costumes," added Mr Spangly, helpfully.

"Training," contributed a penguin.

"Straw to sleep on. . ."

Macabre shook his head with all the indignation he could muster. "Well don't worry, they'll pay for throwing it all back in my face!"

If you had been an enthusiastic trainspotter like young Lucas Fortune, on that dark autumn day, then you would probably have seen the same train as he did, repeatedly criss-crossing the county, the same forbidding shadow as it hissed and roared from station to station with its evil clown's face and gleaming lights.

The Great Macabre eyed the fat creamy moon as it slid down below the pine trees.

"Tomorrow it will be Halloween, our last chance to catch those ungrateful urchins before the boat sails." He grabbed Mr Spangly by his pianokeyboard-patterned lapels and slowly raised him from the floor. "Make sure everyone knows what is required of them. Make certain that they know what the future holds if they fail. And send me the witch, Badhagg. I want to look into that crystal ball of hers again. It is almost Halloween, a time when all the dark things of the world are said to thrive. Let us make it so!!"

CHAPTER SEVENTEEN

A Father's Search Continues

The road ahead of Barrabas stretched far into the distance. The soles of his wellington boots were worn through and he could feel the chill of autumn turning his feet to ice.

Away from his beloved ocean he wasn't much of a navigator. Here there were no rocks, no reefs, no cliffs to guide his path. Even the stars were blotted out by a foul mist.

He tried to make the time spent walking pass more quickly by imagining his missing twins. How would they look now? Would they resemble his dear-departed wife or Barrabas himself? He hoped it was the former.

The slope on which he'd been marching began to level out and there beyond him a little cluster of lights announced his arrival at a new town.

He'd gathered intelligence about all the printing presses in the county and this seemed to be the most promising town in which to look. He examined the fragment of circus poster as he'd examined it a thousand times before and wondered if anyone would recognize it. The legendary patience of Barrabas

O'Hanlon had begun to seep away. He quickened his stride and tried to find his bearings in this strange new locale. . .

CHAPTER EIGHTEEN

Charles Dickins, Printers

Barrabas O'Hanlon paused on the third floor of the rickety staircase. He wasn't out of breath, after all he was used to climbing much steeper staircases than this, no, he had paused to try and find the fragment of paper he'd found at the hospital. There it was, tucked into the pocket of his jacket along with a picture of the twins, a locket of his late wife's hair, and a boiled sweet. A sign on the blackened-out door read:

CHARLES DICKINS, PRINTERS

Barrabas knocked, loudly, and entered. Inside he found semi-darkness and noise, machineclatter and inksmell. Coming towards him was a small man, eyes screwed up, balding and shrewd.

"How can I help you, mister?" he asked.

"Barrabas O'Hanlon," announced the lighthouse keeper, holding out a hand.

"You'll have to speak up, sonny," replied the old man. "Can't hear with the machinery. You'll have to be quick, I got a paper to print by noon."

Barrabas wasn't used to being quick. He fumbled in his pocket for the torn sheet.

"I, I wondered if you remembered having printed this?"

Mr Dickins (for it was he) scratched his head, clicked his tongue, and shook his head uncertainly.

"If you want changes, you're a little late. This was printed nine, ten years ago. You can tell from the type. We don't use that font any more."

The lighthouse keeper's heart skipped a beat.

*C*HUGACHUGACHUGA clattered the printing press. It sounded in time to his own heart.

"I wondered . . . I hoped . . . you might recall for whom you printed this?"

No answer.

*C*HUGACHUGACHUGA.

"I gotta think," said the old printer, dashing off to attend to his press. Barrabas noted a large black cat asleep beneath the machinery. He wondered how it could sleep amidst all this noise.

He glanced at the newspaper as it ran up and down the rollers of the giant press:

```
Lion escape latest! Police cordon
closes in.
```

The outside world was certainly a dangerous place. He thought of Cuthbert and Fatima and hoped they were somewhere safe. Somewhere far from lions and police cordons.

Mr Dickins loomed beside him.

"I remember now. I remember this well. . ." He stared down at the fragment of paper. "I always remember when I don't get paid." His eyes screwed up again. "You got anything to do with this outfit?"

Barrabas shook his head.

"So why d'you wanna find 'em?" asked the printer, thinking himself very smart.

Barrabas produced the picture of his missing tots and began to tell the whole sad tale.

Mr Dickins listened, only vanishing now and then, to check the presses or to add more ink, or to correct a spelling mistake.

"That's some sad story," concluded Dickins, when Barrabas had finished. "I remember the case well. It ran and ran but they never did find those kids – uh, your kids—"

"But now I have a clue," interrupted Barrabas.

Mr Dickins looked down at the paper again. "The guy who ordered this was a clown."

"A clown?"

"Yeah. And a pretty mean one at that. Tried to squirt me in the eye with his flower."

Barrabas cast his mind back to the finding of the old poster. Could a circus performer have visited to entertain the tots? It wasn't impossible.

"Can you remember the name of the circus that ordered this poster?" stammered the lighthouse keeper turned detective.

Mr Dickins rustled through some old papers.

"Not sure what kind of a show it was, but the name was Macabre."

"In what way?"

"No, the name of the circus was *Macabre*. Macabre's Circus."

Barrabas played with the name in his mind. It had a most unpromising ring to it. Not wishing to dwell on his misgivings, the lighthouse keeper thanked Mr Dickins for his help and turned to go. Then turned back again. It was always worth asking.

"I don't suppose you know where the circus is right now?"

Mr Dickins shook his head. "Sorry."

As Barrabas was leaving, head down, shoulders hunched, a voice suddenly called out above the chugachugachug of the machinery. It was Mr Dickins again.

'Try the area round Windflower. I heard they were headed there this week. Say, if you see them, tell 'em I still ain't been paid."

"Thanks. I will," answered Barrabas, his heart skipping with new hope. Was this the end of his search at last?

CHAPTER NINETEEN

Windflower, Halloween Afternoon

Lisa Palermo, local schoolteacher, aged twenty-five, birth sign Virgo, was driving back home in her battered old Pontiac Convertible. She knew she'd left it late for a Halloween costume, but was still hoping she might be able to pull a favour from her old friend, Les McAffrey. He kept a few costumes at the back of his store for special occasions.

The shop was empty when she went in. Lisa couldn't resist trying on a mask hanging on one of the stands. It was Frankenstein's monster.

"Hey, Lisa," smiled Les, appearing with a bacon roll in one hand. "You've had your hair done."

"Very funny, Les." Lisa took off the mask. "Too horrific for the smaller kids. I want a witch's costume or something like that."

Les shook his head. "Sorry, you missed all the good stuff. The last witch walked outta here yesterday."

Lisa looked disappointed. "Got any Pumpkin-headed Goblins?"

"Sorry." Les scratched his head and pointed to an almost empty rail. "All I have left is Frankenstein's monster and this cop costume."

"A cop costume? For Halloween?"

Les gave a wheezy chuckle and swallowed the last of his bacon sandwich. "It's better than nothing. And since you're a pal I'll throw in the cuffs for free."

Lisa turned her nose up and sucked in her teeth. "We-ll, I suppose it might do. Can I try it on?"

"Sure," nodded Les, pointing to a dingy changing room.

MY TEACHER by SADIE FINKLE (8)

My teacher is called Miss Lisa Palermo and she teaches grade four. She is a very nice teacher because she always tries to help us but she also does funny things like taking us camping to look for ghosts and organizing a big Halloween party. Evrybody in our class likes Miss Palermo because she is very brite and knows everything about history and art and she can speak two languages because her family came from Italy many years ago.

Lisa pulled on the police cap and gave herself another look in the mirror, before emerging into the shop and asking Les what he thought.

"It's pretty boring, isn't it?"

Les made a face like he had bubblegum trapped in his teeth. "Mmm. But then they do say all the nice boys like a girl in uniform. Just as long as you don't use those handcuffs on me."

Lisa giggled and reached into her purse. "OK, Les,

73

you sold it to me. I'm a cop for Halloween."

"Want me to wrap it?"

"Actually no. I don't think I've got time. I gotta hook up with the school bus at five. I'll just drive back like this if that's OK by you?"

"Sure, no problem. That'll be twenty buckaroos."

By the time Lisa walked out of the store, the big clock at the end of the street was showing four forty-five p.m., and she was already running late.

CHAPTER TWENTY

More Detective Work

DOGSTOOTH TIMES
NO SIGN OF VANISHED MOPPETS!

Police have revealed that there have been no new developments in the tragic case of kidnapped twins, Cuthbert and Fatima O'Hanlon. The investigation is being wound down, but members of the public are asked to keep their eyes and ears open.

L isa Palermo found the police uniform very itchy.

"Maybe I shouldn't have bothered with this dumb costume," she started to wonder.

On leaving the store she noticed Daniel Liznik (aged 7) crossing the road.

"Hi, Danny."

"Hi, Miss Palermo, I like your outfit."

"Wanna lift?"

"No thanks."

Danny was wearing a skeleton costume. All ready for Halloween. Cute. Lisa waited at the level crossing for a goods train to pass, then glanced at her watch again. She was running *so* late for the party. She thought for a minute or two about going straight there, but then remembered that she had food to collect and a set of false fangs for Elmer Cutschy, who was going dressed as a Vampire.

As she pulled into her driveway minutes later, Lisa was surprised to see a window open on the ground floor, and blinds blowing wildly in the breeze. Even more surprising was the sight of a man climbing out of the window. He appeared to be holding a television set. *Her* television set. A second man landed on the concrete footpath. As he fell, an involuntary spin brought him to rest a few feet away from Lisa. Looking up, the first thing he saw was her police costume.

"Shoot, Charlie," he grumbled to his colleague, "That's the fastest we ever been arrested!"

POLICE STATEMENT OF:
CHARLIE "BIGBIRD" BUKOWSKI

WE WERE PASSING BY THE LADY'S APARTMENT WHEN WE SEE'D A WINDOW OPEN, SO RAY SAYS WHY DON'T WE TAKE A LOOK INSIDE. JUST TO SEE HOW THE LADY ARRANGES HER THINGS LIKE, 'COS RAY IS INTERESTED IN SUCH MATTERS. THEN WHEN WE GOT INSIDE WE SEES THIS TV AND SO RAY SAYS, THAT TV LOOKS PRETTY HEAVY BET YOU COULDN'T LIFT IT. WE WAS JUST TRYIN TO SEE WHO IS THE STRONGEST BETWEEN US WHEN THE LADY CAME IN. IT IS OUR BAD LUCK SHE WAS A COP AND SEEN THINGS ALL WRONG.

POLICE STATEMENT OF:
RAY GUNN

WE STOLE MISS PALERMO'S TELEVISION AND WE WERE GONNA STEAL HER OTHER STUFF TOO. I'M VERY SORRY FOR WHAT WE DONE IT WERE ALL CHARLIE'S IDEA. I HOPE SHE WILL FORGIVE US.

On the driveway outside her home, Lisa wondered what to do next. It isn't every day you find two people robbing your house. At first she'd even forgotten that she was wearing the hired police costume. Fortunately it seemed to make a big impression, or maybe that was on account of the toy gun Les had thrown in. Charlie stuck up his arms straight away. His friend Ray wasn't far behind. They seemed almost relieved to be apprehended.

"Lady cops," muttered Charlie. "I always said they were the smartest."

Lisa was glad the costume had included a set of handcuffs: she hoped they worked.

"C'mon, boys, keep 'em up there," she shouted, trying to sound professional. The handcuffs did their job well enough, though she was pretty sure they were only made from plastic. Charlie was even kind enough to show her how they worked.

"New to the job?" he smiled.

"Yeah, sort of." She ushered the two thieves into the back of her car and told them to put their seat belts on. They obeyed good-naturedly, even though it wasn't easy with handcuffs.

As Lisa turned the ignition key, a large black balloon blew past the windscreen. Written on the side of it, in large white letters, she read:

MACABRE'S TRAVELLING CIRCUS
FOR SPILLS AND THRILLS

At that moment something in the air made her shiver, and it wasn't just the sea-fret that had begun to drift up from the nearby ocean.

"OK, boys, let's get you to the station. . ."

CHAPTER TWENTY-ONE

The Long Arm of the Law

Cuthbert and Fatima were making good progress. Or at least as good as could be expected for two small children mounted on pogo-sticks and carrying impossibly heavy bags. The countryside around them was entirely unfamiliar, but Cuthbert continued to have a finely tuned instinct for the direction in which they should be headed.

The road they were travelling along was of the long and winding variety. It took them past dense clumps of everglade and forest then down into damp, foggy hollows. Meanwhile, at the other end of the very same road, Highway Number 11, a man was driving a large white car. His name was Sheriff Cohnberg, and he was on his way from Windflower to a small farm on the prairie, where there'd been a report of two strange figures on the prowl.

TRANSCRIPT RADIO MESSAGE FROM OFFICER COHNBERG TO HQ

"That you, Harry?"

"Roger."

"Please state your position."

"I'm sitting down, Bill."

"Very funny, Harry."

"OK. I'm on Highway 11. No sign of anyone around so far. Not that you can see much in this fog. The kids gotta fine night for Halloween all right. . ."

"You said it. Gimme a call if you see anything."

"Check."

Sheriff Cohnberg had no sooner put down his radio than he saw something approaching along the other side of the road. He screwed up his eyes. It was hard to see anything in that mist. If he didn't know better he would have said it was two kids on pogo-sticks dressed as Indians. Time to get an eye test.

Fatima blew a sigh of relief. "Did you see that? Someone in a car. Was he looking for us?"

Cuthbert dismounted from his pogo-stick and stared back down the road, shrouded in mist.

"It's time we got off this road," continued his sister. "Too busy."

Cuthbert was in full agreement. "One does not want to make the acquaintance of strangers at this time of day."

It was still only 4.30 p.m., but Fatima knew what

80

her brother meant.

Suddenly they heard the sound of a car reversing back towards them, then from out of the mist, a voice calling out, "Hey! Kids!"

Fatima looked up, heart pounding. They were stranded by the side of the road, no time to hide.

"It's a rough night. Fancy a lift?"

Cuthbert and Fatima peered into the gloom. They still couldn't see anyone. Suddenly, looming before them, stood the sheriff. He took off his hat and smiled.

"Great masks. Get those for Halloween?"

"We aren't wearing masks," answered Cuthbert.

The sheriff chuckled. "Sure, sure, hee-hee, you jokers! Hop in the back. Now where can I take you?"

Misinterpreting the sheriff's kindly actions as a kidnap attempt, the Gruesome Twosome suddenly made a bolt for it. They remounted their pogo-sticks and bounced off as fast as they could towards the dark and gloomy forest, not once stopping to look behind, even when distant car headlights criss-crossed their path like search beacons.

They reached the heart of the wood and paused for a moment, hearts pounding.

"Has he gone?"

"I hope so. . ."

Back on the highway, the sheriff scratched his head. Maybe he *had* been seeing things? The two kids had vanished without trace. From deep in the forest came a loud and unearthly rumble. It sounded like thunder but it wasn't. Sheriff Cohnberg climbed back into his patrol car, unaware of the dark forces drawing in around him.

At much the same time, Cuthbert and Fatima were concealed in the foggy embrace of the everglades and turning their thoughts once more towards Windflower and what they hoped would be safety.

CHAPTER TWENTY-TWO

The Witch and the Ringmaster

Elsewhere that Halloween afternoon, a train whistle pierced the gloom. The old signalman couldn't believe his eyes. A train couldn't be travelling so fast towards him, not when it was heading in the wrong direction! He glimpsed the hideous figure of the fire-eater, leaning out of a carriage window, blowing jets of flame into the night air. The sparks leaped towards his signal box and the old man had to throw himself under a table. From there he could hear the carriages as they rattled and clattered past, and a blood-curdling roar that sounded to his frightened ears like hungry lions.

Inside the speeding train, Macabre had pressed Badhagg's head against her crystal ball. "Where are they?" he snarled. "Where are the runaways?"

Badhagg flourished long skinny hands across the glass of the crystal ball and slowly the mists began to clear. For a moment, everything inside the glass was real and everything in the real world became as glass. . .

"It's very misty. Hard to see."

The old witch's eyes flickered from side to side like

two tadpoles in a cloudy stream. She raised her spindly finger to the glass and pointed.

"There! There are your runaways!"

Macabre's teeth widened into a grin, like the barrels of a fairground organ. Badhagg's finger was pointing to a signpost, half covered by nettles and mist. It stood by the side of a small road. Though the lettering had begun to fade after years of wind and rain, a name could still be read. And the name was "Windflower". The same Windflower where Mrs Hubbard lived, where Lisa Palermo had just hired her costume, and towards which Sheriff Cohnberg was driving his patrol car down the Halloween-fogged highway. . .

CHAPTER TWENTY-THREE

> ## THE WINDFLOWER ACADEMY FOR CHILDREN'S EDUCATION AND BETTERMENT
>
> ---
>
> WE WELCOME CHILDREN OF ALL AGES, HEIGHTS, AND ABILITIES.
> OUR AIM IS TO CREATE THE MODEL CITIZENS OF THE FUTURE.
>
> ## MAXIMA OMNIUM ADMIRATIONE
> TO THE ASTONISHMENT OF ALL

"Children! In line please! Charlie Tenenbloom, put down that giant pumpkin!" Mrs Kernowitz was struggling to make her voice heard. This was Miss Palermo's class and they didn't seem to take any notice of anyone else.

Outside the school gates a disordered mob of around twenty kids was now scrambling towards the school bus, dressed in a variety of Halloween costumes. The class were en route to a special Trick-or-Treat party and their high-pitched excited chatter pierced the air. Lisa Palermo should have been there to see them on to the bus but for some reason she seemed to have been delayed. Mrs Kernowitz blew her whistle in a vain attempt to bring some sense of order. . .

Lisa parked up by the side of the road right in front of the police station. She wondered about going inside whilst still dressed in her police costume, but had the feeling it was probably illegal to go round dressed as a cop. On the other hand she was running late for her Halloween party and still had the two criminals to get rid of. Hopefully there wouldn't be too much red tape involved.

The station was quiet. Windflower wasn't exactly the crime capital of the world. Aside from Sheriff Cohnberg there were only two other law officers in town: Officer Mary Montgomery, and Sergeant Ed Gilbert. Since Mary was off on holiday with her kids, it fell to Sergeant Gilbert to deal with Lisa's two hoodlums. He licked the end of his pen and began to write. . .

REPORT OF SGT GILBERT

DATE:
TIME:
OFFICER ON DUTY: SGT. E. GILBERT

INITIAL REPORT: TWO SUSPECTS BROUGHT IN
UNDER SUSPICION OF ROBBERY.

NAMES: NAMES OF BUKOWSKI AND GUNN. BROUGHT IN
BY MISS L PALERMO. LOCAL TEACHER.
BUKOWSKI AND GUNN REQUESTED A LAWYER. MISS
PALERMO REQUESTED THAT SHE BE ALLOWED TO
MAKE HER STATEMENT LATER ON ACCOUNT OF BEING
LATE FOR A SCHOOL FUNCTION. SINCE SHE HAD TO
TAKE CARE OF YOUNG PERSONS AT THIS TIME I
AGREED WITH HER REQUEST ON CONDITION THAT
SHE WOULD RETURN BY 10 P.M. TONIGHT AT THE
LATEST.

PRISONERS' POSSESSIONS: THE POCKETS OF
PRISONER BUKOWSKI WERE COMPLETELY EMPTY.
PRISONER GUNN'S POCKETS CONTAINED TWELVE CENTS
AND A BUBBLEGUM CARD SHOWING A COMIC BOOK
CHARACTER (BELIEVED TO BE BATMAN). THE
PRISONERS WAS LOCKED IN THEIR CELLS PENDING
FURTHER INVESTIGATIONS AT 5.55 P.M.

SIGNED:

E.GILBERT
DUTY OFFICER.

Lisa glanced at her watch for the hundredth time that evening. She was due to rendezvous with the school bus fifteen minutes ago!

Meanwhile, on that same school bus, there were twenty kids in Halloween costumes. Twenty kids as high as kites. Driver Abel Doodlebug was beginning to look more than a little flustered. Where was Miss Palermo? And why had she left him alone with these hyperactive, Halloween-crazed high-schoolers?

He gave a second look at the clock alongside his driving mirror, took out his earplugs, and tried to make himself heard above the excited din.

"Look, kids, can we keep da noise down?"

An empty carton of fries flew past his left ear.

"No, listen up, PLEASE!"

For a moment, the din subsided.

"It looks like Miss Palermo ain't gonna make it."

There were groans from all along the bus. Two junior werewolves looked like they were about to burst into tears. Driver Doodlebug didn't like kids much, but he didn't like to see them cry either. Against his better judgement he decided to make them an offer.

"Look, since it's Halloween and I know you kids is all dressed up, if she don't show in the next five minutes, I'll take you all up to Mrs Hubbard's myself. And you can—"

The cheering started.

"—And you can still have your party. . ."

Chaos broke out once more. Driver Doodlebug was suddenly the most popular man in Windflower. He

The Windflower Coach Company

For all your travel needs.

* School Parties a specialty *

<u>Fully insured</u>

Contact Mr and Mrs Doodlebug

Windflower 959559

put his earplugs in once more and hoped that some-how there would be a miracle and Lisa Palermo might still appear.

Five minutes later, Driver Doodlebug turned on the engine and reversed out of the car park. The kids were on their way to Mrs Hubbard's Halloween party. He had lost one of his earplugs and now was hoping that the sound from his radio was loud enough to drown out their high-pitched squeals of excitement.

By the time Lisa arrived at the rendezvous spot there was no sign of either the coach or the kids.

CHAPTER TWENTY-FOUR

A Second Escape

Some miles hence, Cuthbert and Fatima had dismounted from their pogo-sticks for a moment. They were sure that Sheriff Cohnberg and his police car couldn't be far off. A timber sign wreathed in fog pointed to a distant town. The writing on the sign was worn but still legible. "Windflower", it read. "Three miles".

"It still looks a nice spot," exclaimed Fatima, peering into the distant haze. "Though I don't remember much apart from Mrs Hubbard's house and the graveyard."

"I always liked that it was beside the sea."

Fatima nodded. "Me too. Though I don't know why that should make any difference." A gust of breeze picked up and ruffled her hair. "Doesn't freedom feel good?"

"It certainly does," agreed Cuthbert, breathing in the air and stretching out his long, skinny arms.

For a moment the twins could enjoy the peace and quiet of the countryside. In the distance the sea murmured peacefully. Windruffle and near silence. But then Fatima cocked her head to one side.

"I hear an engine. . ."

"The sheriff?" Cuthbert crouched down behind the road sign.

Fatima shook her head. "No."

Cuthbert's eyes grew wide with fear. "Macabre?"

Without speaking the twins retreated back into the undergrowth, clutching their pogo-sticks.

"I don't think it's him. But we should take no chances." Fatima produced two cloaks from out of her bag and wrapped one of them around her sibling until he looked like a giant frightened owl. "Don't move!" she whispered, throwing the second cloak over herself.

Now the noise was almost upon them. Seconds later, the Windflower school bus crept past, driven by Abel Doodlebug and lost in the fog. The only person to notice Cuthbert and Fatima crouching down in the bushes was Daniel Liznik.

"Hey! Two giant owls!" he shouted. But no one took any notice. They were all too excited about Mrs Hubbard's Halloween party.

There was a pause before Cuthbert asked if it was safe to come out from under his cloak.

Fatima removed the cloak with a circus-like flourish and watched as her brother climbed back on to his pogo-stick. "Let us repair to Windflower, thence to ask directions. 22a, Gravestone Walk is the house we seek."

"It sounds like home already," added Cuthbert, hopefully.

And for a while, all that could be seen in that silvery, twilit landscape was the sight of two tiny figures on pogo-sticks, bouncing off towards the town of Windflower and the great grey ocean beyond.

CHAPTER TWENTY-FIVE

A Warm and Familiar Place

22a Gravestone Walk had once been a magnificent mansion. Now it was a magnificent, but *crumbling* mansion. Built originally for the famous dynamite tycoon, J T Doodlebug, it had been inherited by his only daughter, old Mrs Hubbard. She had always wanted to retire to her childhood home by the sea with her memories and collection of cats. Now, years later, the memories were fading and only one of the cats remained, a rather sour-tempered individual called Oliver.

The house lay a little way out of town. It overlooked Windflower graveyard on three sides, whilst on the other, a thin strip of long overgrown grass led down to the river. It looked so ramshackle that a breath of wind might blow it down, but fortunately this was far from being the case. Dynamite millionaires build things to last, and so it had proved with number 22a. All through the winter, storms would blow up from the sea and batter hard against its timbers and tiles, but still Mrs Hubbard's house stood the test of time.

The old lady was in the kitchen baking gingerbread men. "The children will enjoy these cookies, don't you think?" she smiled, addressing Oliver, her cat.

The latter had positioned himself by the side of the oven, and been forced to wear a bright yellow paper party hat. Like the Great Macabre, Oliver didn't like parties. Mrs Hubbard found it hard to imagine anyone not liking parties, especially not Halloween parties. She held one every year, for the local kids.

THE WINDFLOWER WEEKLY NEWS
WIDOW TO TREAT KIDS

The lucky children of Windflower will once again be invited to a special Halloween Party to be held at the home of the town's oldest inhabitant. Mrs Amelia Hubbard, 107, says that she hopes this year's party will be the biggest ever. Over twenty children have been invited and they are expected to consume over a hundred cakes during the course of the evening.

"Keep an eye on these gingerbread men, Oliver, whilst I change into my best frock."

Oliver blinked his eyes slowly and watched as the hands of the old clock on the wall moved towards six o'clock. Oliver was both discreet and patient. He put up with Mrs Hubbard's fussing and foolishness because it suited him – for now. . .

CHAPTER TWENTY-SIX

Black Balloons at a Small Station

Mr Spangly was crying as usual. Great torrents of tears ran into a bucket which he himself was holding. Mr Spangly did a lot of crying. It was part of his act and he liked to get in as much practise as possible.

Macabre swaggered down the carriage, checking for laughter or signs of light-heartedness. He turned and snapped at the Remarkable Otto.

"Where did the witch go? I ordered her to track the runaways!"

The strongman stammered out a reply as best he could. "S-she said it v-vas H-Halloween and she vanted to check it out. . ."

A great cloud of black steam suddenly issued forth from the train's funnel, followed by a blast from a siren. The train plunged through a long tunnel, and when it re-emerged a sign by the side of the track announced its arrival outside the town of Windflower. To commemorate this happy event, Macabre ordered his helpers to release a second bunch of black balloons into the night air.

"What a Halloween this will be," he chuckled.

"The Gruesome Twosome's little holiday is over and soon they'll be back here where they belong!"

"Back here where they belong," gloated the clowns, penguins and assorted performers of that terrible circus.

The mist cloaking the countryside had slowly begun to clear and from low in the sky, the moon glinted its autumnal beam over the woods and hollows that skirted Windflower. The Carnival Train gave another piercing shriek from its whistle and thundered on.

It had already been a long day for Abel. And it was about to get even longer. The school bus was grinding its way along Minever Drive, when a cloud of steam began to pour out from the engine.

Behind him, it was bedlam.

"Look, kids, can you cool it a minute?" he shouted, more in hope than in expectation. An apple core narrowly missed his head. "I hope you ain't gonna behave like this when we get to Mrs Hubbard's!"

Two kids in ghoul costumes were wrestling each other on the floor of the bus. As Abel looked out, his view of the way ahead was now completely obscured by great clouds of billowing bluish-grey smoke. He had no option but to pull over and switch off the engine.

For a moment there was a pause in the hullabaloo.

"Hey, what's going on?" asked Jimmy Petrie (10).

Driver Doodlebug was already on the two-way

radio, trying to contact his wife, who knew more about engines than he did. "Hello . . . this is honey-bee to home hive . . . do you read me?"

A great burst of interference almost deafened poor Abel and he was forced to hold the receiver away from his ear. He mopped his brow. If he couldn't get these kids to Mrs Hubbard's soon then he feared a revolt. And he had seen enough revolting children for one day.

"Hello – home hive – do-you-read-me? We have a problem here."

They say strange things do happen on the witching night. Was it just coincidence that Abel Doodlebug's coach had broken down, that burglars were on the prowl, that lights had gone out in the town hall, and that all phone lines in Windflower were now dead?

At the very instant when every street of the town should have been filled with the sight and sounds of trick-or-treaters, there was actually a very spooky silence. Or rather, near-silence. For if anyone had listened very hard, they might well have detected, in the distance, the sound of a train, rumbling across frosted fields and byways, the shriek of a whistle, the roar of unfed beasts. Even Mrs Hubbard, baking gingerbread men, felt a shiver run down her elderly spine.

CHAPTER TWENTY-SEVEN

More Arrivals

BOING, BOING, BOING. . . Coming closer. . . Two pogo-sticks in need of an oiling bouncing along. Cuthbert and Fatima emerged from the everglades to the crest of a small hill. Behind them they could see Abel Doodlebug's school bus, stranded by the side of the road. Fatima motioned to Cuthbert to crouch down while they watched.

"Those children look like they're having fun. Do you suppose we were ever like that?"

Cuthbert thought for a moment. "I recall no such time."

"Perhaps Windflower will be our new home?" Fatima wondered out loud. "Maybe one day we too will go to school in a bus like that?"

"Perhaps. Maybe. It is nice to have somewhere-over the-rainbow dreams."

Looking ahead, the road now forked in two.

Fatima glanced first to the left and then to the right. "If only we had a map. 'Gravestone Walk' is where the lady lived. Cuthbert, keep your eyes peeled for a graveyard."

"Mine eyes are peeled," replied her brother, drily.

"So . . . left or right?" Fatima turned to the right.

Cuthbert sniffed the air, which was a weird mixture of sea, fresh pumpkin, and diesel from the school bus. "Let us follow our hearts," he announced and, without hesitating, turned to the left.

Fatima could see, half-hidden by the deepening twilight, a large wooden fairground, topped with a giant roller-coaster ride. Something about that sight sent a shiver down her spine. It reminded her of circuses.

Cuthbert slowed his progress until Fatima was alongside, and then they continued to pogo up the hill.

"Long road!" puffed Fatima, rosy-cheeked with effort.

"A long and winding road," her twin agreed.

After exploring the outskirts of the town, Cuthbert's instincts drew him to a hilly suburb where the houses were large and the trees forbidding. It was Fatima who noticed, eventually, a sign at the side of the road. "1-700 Gravestone Walk", it read.

Silver tears glistened in Fatima's eyes. "I hope she is as kind as we remember her."

"She gave us cookies," answered Cuthbert without hesitation. "And it was warm and sunny."

Fatima nodded and they continued on their way with a mixture of excitement and exhaustion, for travelling long distances by pogo-stick is not really to be recommended. . .

On the other side of town a dark and rusted locomotive

was rattling along a rusted track. At the front of its engine grinned a hideous clown.

The ringmaster jerked back a curtain and peered out. "How far are we from our destination? Is this it? Is this Windflower?"

An army of strange heads looked out, surveying the scene.

"You should never look out of a train window when it's moving," warned Badhagg.

"Who asked you?" hissed Macabre, continuing to peer down the track. The train was now entering a tunnel, the sound of its engine suddenly much louder. By the time the train had emerged from the other end, Macabre's normally pallid features were caked with thick layers of black soot. All except for the eyes. Mr Spangly had to bite his tongue to stop laughing.

Badhagg's crystal ball began to glow again. Tiny frosted stars melting from the side of the glass before turning to mist, which in turn cleared to reveal the image of a winding road lined with ancient, crumbling mansions.

Badhagg smiled with dry, cracked lips. "We're so close I can almost hear their tiny hearts beating with fear."

"Good!" growled Macabre, wiping his sooty features with a silk handkerchief.

"Reduce speed, Mr Spangly!"

The tearful clown nodded and rushed off down the compartment towards the engine car. Seconds later there was a sudden hiss of steam, a grinding of well-worn brakes, and then finally, a long, juddering motion that lasted for close on a minute.

Macabre's train had arrived in town!

CHAPTER TWENTY-EIGHT

A Large Mammal Faces Arrest

Not far away, Sheriff Cohnberg had almost finished his shift. His weird encounter with the two vanishing Native American kids had left him in need of a stiff coffee, and he was glad to be on the road home. The route up ahead appeared quiet, his headlights revealing nothing more than a thick layer of mist across the highway. He had just begun to whistle a tune to himself when he saw something which made him squint his eyes in disbelief. There was a train blocking the road!

At the same moment, the driver of that very train, a brown bear from the Caucasian Mountains (whose circus act consisted mainly of balancing on a large red ball) was staring out of the window of his cabin, awaiting instructions from Macabre. The bear proved equally surprised to find itself face to face with Sheriff Harry Cohnberg.

The latter was now eyeing the train up and down. If he was shocked to find a bear in charge of such a large locomotive, then he tried not to show it.

"Illegal parking on a State Highway," he said to himself, just loudly enough that the bear would hear too. "Bear in charge of a train . . . not sure that's legal and even if it is, then it shouldn't be . . . get Bill to look into that one." Each time he thought of a possible offence, he dictated it into a small hand-held tape recorder which he was holding just above his left breast-pocket.

Further down the train, Macabre was spluttering with Outrage. Outrage was one of his clown body-guards, a tall, sad-looking individual with limegreen hair and an inflatable tie.

"Why have we stopped?" snarled the red-faced ringmaster, his eyes bulging with anger. "I said reduce speed, not come to a complete halt!"

Outrage looked out of the window. "It's the law."

"The law!" Macabre cocked his head to one side as if trying to recall some incident from his murky past. "But we've done nothing wrong," he whined. "Not yet. We only just arrived!"

Mr Spangly began to cry again. "Nobody likes the circus."

"We'll see about that!" snapped Macabre, flinging open the door of his compartment. The mist swirled about his knee-length leather boots. In the distance, Sheriff Cohnberg was still checking the train for possible defects while the bear listened, unconcerned.

"I don't care for the look of those wheel bearings . . . and I'll need to see your permits for the wild animals. . ."

Seeing that the bear displayed no interest in what

he was saying, the sheriff looked around for another figure of authority. He turned to find a huge figure towering over him.

There was a blood-red frock coat buttoned tightly over a shimmering silk shirt. Beneath that, a pair of extravagantly shaped jodhpurs, tucked into shining leather boots. But the crowning glory of Macabre's outfit was his top hat. Its dazzling height seemed to vanish upwards to the sky and was made of something resembling black sealskin.

"Finian Macabre, Ringmaster. How may I help, officer? Is there a problem?"

The sheriff took an involuntary step back, but he was a country boy, laid-back and hard to shock, not the type to let things bother him. He regained his composure and took out his notepad.

"Good evening, sir. Is this vehicle registered in your name?"

Macabre smiled his green-toothed smile. For a second the sheriff had to look away.

"It has been in my family for generations. Thirteen generations to be precise!"

"Thirteen generations? That would be approximately how many years?"

"Since 1692," replied Macabre, without missing a beat.

The sheriff scratched his head. "I didn't know they had locos back then."

"I'm sure there's a lot you don't know," smirked Macabre.

"So you are the registered keeper?" continued the lawman, doggedly.

"The keeper is with his lions. Would you like to meet him?"

Something about Macabre's expression during their interview made the sheriff feel like he was being toyed with. When the ringmaster smiled, Sheriff Cohnberg noticed that he had a single silver tooth amongst all the rows of decaying green. And those eyes! He didn't ever recall seeing eyes quite so . . . red. . .

"Does this bear have a current licence?" the lawman asked.

Macabre didn't answer at first, but gave another smirk. "No, but he has a currant bun."

Macabre's clown bodyguards (who were now gathered about him) erupted into high-pitched laughter. Sheriff Cohnberg felt his collar uneasily. The whole evening was beginning to get to him. First there'd been the strange trick-or-treaters who'd vanished into the forest. And now there was this weird train, driven by a bear, and run by a madman in a top hat. Whoever these people were, he didn't want them coming anywhere near Windflower.

"Do you plan on setting up your show here, sir?"

"We may be here a few days."

It was then that the sheriff made the fatal mistake of taking Ringmaster Macabre to one side. "I think, just between you and me, it might be better if you moved your train on someplace else. We got our own show in Windflower you see."

Macabre's eyes narrowed, unpleasantly. "Your own show?"

The sheriff nodded, already wishing he hadn't said anything. "Er, yeah . . . we have a fairground down by the seashore."

"But Macabre's Circus is the FINEST in the world!"

The sheriff shrugged his shoulders (mistake number two). "I think you'll find we folks round here prefer our own local entertainment."

Mr Spangly, watching from afar, thought that Macabre might actually burst, so red had his cheeks grown.

"The fairground hasn't been built which can match my show!" he snarled.

Sheriff Cohnberg puffed out his cheeks and spat into a nearby puddle. He was getting tired of all this and wanted to go home.

"Your little fairground must be magic, Sheriff, to have such a BEWITCHING effect on people." As he spoke, Macabre winked at Badhagg, who was watching nearby. Badhagg's eyes glinted in reply.

"It's magic all right," nodded the sheriff, unaware that the net was closing in on him.

The Great Macabre span on his heels and gave a deep-throated and unpleasant laugh. "Well, Sheriff – if you like the sound of a magic fairground then I think we can help you—"

An unexplained clap of thunder erupted overhead, making the sheriff jump.

Macabre ushered forth Badhagg and whispered into

her ear. "This fool displeases me! I want you to put this wretched town under a spell. Can you manage that?"

Badhagg frowned. "I wasn't aware I could say no to any of your requests. So sure, make the most of my magic while you can. I'll do you a Halloween spell."

Macabre ignored her sarcastic tone. "Good. Then proceed at once!"

Sheriff Cohnberg turned up the collar of his coat; it seemed all of a sudden to have turned very stormy. Leaves and twigs were blowing around his feet. At first he didn't even notice Badhagg as she raised her arms to the heavens and began muttering a strange, obscure spell.

"Naka, naka, Eowha-Hoo!"

"Is she all right?" asked the lawman, suddenly noticing that the old crone was now hovering a few centimetres off the ground.

"She's fine," smiled Macabre. "This is her favourite time of year. Halloween!"

"What exactly does she do?" enquired the sheriff. "When she's not dressed in that kooky costume?"

Macabre fixed him with an icy gaze. "She's a witch of course!"

Sheriff Cohnberg guessed that this must be a joke, but he was no longer a hundred per cent certain. Not about this, not about anything. These circus people were weird. He decided to radio back to HQ just to keep them up to date. "Bill. . . Hello? Bill . . . can you hear me?"

But there was no response . . . just a dull hum down the line.

Another rumble of thunder echoed overhead.

Badhagg's spell was transforming the whole atmosphere. From out of the carnival train a troupe of sinister penguins emerged and began dancing a graceful pirouette. Sheriff Cohnberg was surprised to see that the penguins were also carrying umbrellas. And no ordinary umbrellas. These were decorated with a swirling black and white pattern, forming a hypnotic spiral. The sheriff swallowed hard and wished his deputy, Bill, would arrive with some backup.

In front of him the penguins were now dancing in line, twirling their umbrellas as they went.

Sheriff Cohnberg felt his eyes growing heavy. "Got to . . . keep . . . awake –" he mumbled, as his notebook and pen dropped from his hands. The air filled with a strange enchanting music; it reminded him of an out-of-tune music box his mother once owned. The sheriff's eyes grew white and round, like two china saucers from Les's hardware store.

"I must go to the fairground," he was now mumbling, in a monotonous voice. "It will be magic and fun." He wandered off, clearly not himself.

The Great Macabre clapped his hands together in delight. "This is a good beginning to our night's work, but only a beginning. I want everyone from this town to enjoy the delights of their precious fairground the same as that fool of a sheriff."

Badhagg nodded and started to intone another spell . . .

All of Windflower born
Fall under my spell till morn.
From age of a hundred down to one,
All your will power now is gone.
To the fairground make your way
Within its grounds you'll want to stay,
if not for ever,
then to the first break of day.

Hands clapped. Lightning flashed. A foul smell. Sulphur burned. In an instant, the witch's work was done and she retreated to the Carnival Train to lie down.

Macabre continued to address the rest of his circus army, "The witch has cleared the streets of this dismal town. Now we must find those knife-throwing miscreants. Our ship leaves for the East in a day's time and we must have them under lock and key by the end of the night. So go and do your worst!"

As one the circus folk melted into the gloom. Horns tooted and umbrellas twirled. The search for Cuthbert and Fatima had begun in earnest!

CHAPTER TWENTY-NINE

J T DOODLEBUG:
Windflower's most famous citizen,
by Cherry Dempster.

Born in a humble homestead, two miles north of Windflower, Johan Thomas Doodlebug came to be known as "The Father of Explosions", and the man who brought dynamite to the masses.

After a lifetime working in laboratories in the West, J T Doodlebug returned to his home town in order to build a school and help reconstruct the community in which he had grown up.

How many people know that it is to this modest man that we owe the J T Doodlebug town clock, the J T Doodlebug Memorial Hall, and the J T Doodlebug Museum of Controlled Explosions.

Various other sites of interest can be found around the town, including the scene of his last great blasting project, and part of his jawbone.

FATIMA'S DIARY

Windflower. I just want to write about Windflower, in case we don't stay here long. Though of course I hope we do. We have only seen it twice in our lives, but already it seems like somewhere we can call home.

It is situated, very pleasantly, by the sea, which you can generally see from all parts. Especially if mounted on a pogo-stick. There are many wooded areas, filled with pine trees, and so sweet smelling that we have quite forgotten the aroma of popcorn we smelled every day of our lives in the circus.

The town is quite grand. There are shops selling everything you can think of, and at one end of the main street there is a statue of the town's founder, a man called Augustus Windflower. He was the man who invented a powerful explosive called Jellygnite (I think this is how you spell it). He has a very long curled moustache like Macabre, but an altogether kinder countenance.

I will tell you more about Windflower when I have the time, but Cuthbert is tugging at my sleeve and telling me we must hurry on, for it's getting late.

CHAPTER THIRTY

The school bus was still stuck by the side of the road and Abel Doodlebug had run out of ideas. Behind him, the Halloween party kids had gone completely crazy and there was no controlling them. His only hope was that they wouldn't beat up his bus too much.

"C'mon now, folks – show a little respect back there!" As Abel looked down the coach he was surprised to see that a sudden and immediate calm had descended upon the inhabitants of the bus. "That's more like it."

He was surprised they'd paid any attention to him, but glad of the peace and quiet while he tried to call his wife again. "Honey bee to home hive. . . Please come in. . ."

The sound of a hooting car horn suddenly broke his train of thought.

HONK! HONK!

A clown wearing a loud checked jacket was cycling past in front of the bus. The clown's neck, bizarrely, seemed able to rotate 180 degrees in any direction.

"What in tootin' tarnation!" spluttered Abel.

"Come to the fair! Come to the fair!" cried the clown into a large brass megaphone. "There's lots and lots for little kiddietots!"

First to go was Orville Dean, a small hesitant boy with a stammer. He stumbled out of the exit muttering to himself, "I *will* go to the fair. I will forget all my t-troubles and c-cares."

The burly bus driver made to grab Orville by the arm but the youngster was surprisingly strong.

"Wait!" protested Doodlebug. "You can't just go runnin' off to no fair!"

The Leakey Twins were next to push past him, and then Sadie Finkel and Daniel Liznik. It seemed there wasn't a child on board who didn't want to go to the fair right that minute.

Outside, on the mist-shrouded street, children were already intermingling with cycling clowns and a bunch of penguins who twirled patterned umbrellas. As the umbrellas began to spin and the witch's spell took hold, bus driver Doodlebug began to forget all his troubles too. It was as if he were falling into a beautiful dream. It didn't matter any more about the smoking engine. It was an old bus, bound to break down one day. And if the kids wanted to go the fair, what was so wrong about that? Hell, he quite fancied going there himself. Maybe he could even win a coconut for Mrs Doodlebug? And what a fine night it was too. Cold, but not so cold once you began to walk.

Coach driver Doodlebug was now walking down

the road, arms by his side, eyes staring straight ahead of him like two flying saucers. Alongside him ambled Sheriff Cohnberg. He was heading in the same direction with the same lifeless walk. It was like some weird version of *The Pied Piper of Hamlyn*. Except that it wasn't a piper calling the tune, it was clowns on unicycles.

The chaotic procession slowly wound its way down towards the wooden fairground, and at each turn in the road, its number grew. Townsfolk and circus folk mingled as one, but there could be no doubt as to who was leading who. . .

THIS FAIRGROUND WAS OPENED ON
12TH JUNE, 19--
BY
MRS HIRAM DODGEM

IT HAS BEEN CREATED PRIMARILY FOR THE ENJOYMENT OF THE CITIZENS AND CHILDREN OF WINDFLOWER, BUT VISITORS TO OUR TOWN ARE MOST WELCOME TO SHARE ITS PLEASURES.

THE COMMITTEE

The witch Badhagg was studying events from the railway siding where the Carnival Train had come to rest. Macabre stood next to her.

"That was one of the meanest spells I have ever cast," she croaked, as the spellbound folk of Windflower began to wander past with hollow staring eyes. Her laughter was like batsqueak. "Now can I go and enjoy Halloween?"

"You're forgetting the Gruesome Twosome!" hissed Macabre. "We still haven't caught them and that's the most important task of all."

Badhagg knew it was useless to argue, but her eyes didn't hide the resentment she felt. "I'll take my broom and see if I can spot them from on high."

"Why not use your crystal ball?" snapped Macabre.

"Difficult to penetrate that mist," she hissed. But in reality she ached to be airborne on that special night. If it meant tricking Macabre to do so, then so be it.

Badhagg pulled on a set of flying goggles. Her witch's broom roared into life.

Bluesmoke and hotsparks.

Seconds later she was airbound and banking steeply above the railway.

"Do this! Do that!" she muttered once she knew she was out of earshot. "One of these days he won't talk to me like that again! One of these days things can get back to the way they used to be . . . and one of these days is coming real soon! Hahahahaha!"

By now her figure was silhouetted against the night sky and directly below her, Badhagg could just make out the lights of the fairground as Macabre ordered it into life. Levers were pulled, generators whirred, rides began to spin slowly around.

This was now the only sign of activity in that ghostly seaside town, for the ringmaster had also commanded his circus army to sever all telephone lines and electricity supplies. Darkness filled nine-tenths of the neighbourhood, and in that darkness the zombie inhabitants of Windflower walked slowly to the fairground by the sea, drawn by the witch's inexorable spell. . .

CHAPTER THIRTY-ONE

Lisa Alone

After all the delays and bureaucracy at the police station, Lisa's car was now passing near the old fairground. Already she was hopelessly late for Mrs Hubbard's Halloween party. Surely nothing else could go wrong?

There seemed to be a lot of children on the streets that night. Nothing unusual in that she supposed. It was Halloween after all. But why were they all headed for the fairground? Perhaps there was another party she hadn't heard about. In the distance she glimpsed Sheriff Cohnberg. What was he doing walking along, candyfloss in hand? It was unusual ever to see him out of his patrol car.

"Hey! Harry!" she shouted. Lisa could hear footsteps moving nearer to the car. In the driving mirror above her head she watched the sheriff as he stumbled past.

Something about the sheriff's expression made Lisa feel frightened. He looked like a zombie from a horror movie, with his white face and staring eyes, and his arms stretched in front of him. Lisa's heart began to thump as she took in the scene. She felt a cold chill slide down her spine. A sense of something very wrong. She tried to convince herself it might be something to do with Halloween . . . a party or a parade . . . with everyone pretending to be ghouls. But it didn't work. This was no party.

In the sickly grey twilight, lit only by the lights of the various rides, the citizens of Windflower continued to wander past, each as zombified as the sheriff.

Lisa crouched low in her car and watched as clowns twirled down the street, followed by moth-eaten lions, a strongman, a two headed fire-eater, and a whole host of unwholesome characters. Grotesque as they were, their appearance well suited the chilling mood of the fairground that night.

Lisa herself had not fallen under the witch's malevolent spell only on account of not having been born in Windflower, but at Shakespeer Bay, some five and twenty miles north. Badhagg's curse, though terrible, applied only to the locals, although of course Lisa herself was as yet unaware of her good fortune. . .

Despite her instincts telling her to remain hidden, Lisa's mind soon turned to the kids in her class. Were they too inside this creepy fairground? She'd seen one or two children she recognized in the crowds wandering the fairground. Lisa didn't feel she could leave without trying to learn more about what was happening that night. Hopefully her class were safe at Mrs Hubbard's but if not, she needed to know. Dare she get out of her car to find out?

CHAPTER THIRTY-TWO

Graveyard calm, graveyard still,
where ivy scrambles over stones so chill. . .
(poem by the Mayoress of Windflower,
Mrs Annabella Fugg)

Halloween. Two slender figures with deathly white faces, prowling around a thickmisted graveyard.

Jagged, leafless trees framing the view. Quiet. Quiet as a graveyard. Mrs Hubbard's house, number 22a, Gravestone Walk, lay opposite, partially hidden by a giant yew tree, whose dark, rotting branches gave the impression of filling the whole garden.

"Ill-met by moonlight. . ." whispered Cuthbert, as they stood in the shadows, wondering what to do next.

"Don't ramble so," scolded Fatima. "This is serious."

"But I like to ramble," persisted her brother, half hidden by fog.

Fatima was examining the neighbourhood. "This is the graveyard all right."

"And there . . . there stands the old lady's house!"

Fatima nodded. Ahead of them stood a set of iron gates decorated with a familiar pattern, made from entwining sticks of dynamite. There was a faded sign by the side of the gates and now Fatima was close enough to read it, "Mrs Hubbard, 22a, Gravestone Walk."

"Our land of milk and cookies!" whispered Cuthbert, with stars in his eyes.

"I can smell gingerbread in the air," continued Fatima. "Perhaps we are expected?"

The Gruesome Twosome were so tiny compared with the iron gates that it took both twins pushing hard to get them to move. The gates screeched on rusty hinges. The sound reminded them of the Carnival Train, and of the lock on their compartment door when Macabre's clowns slammed it shut each night.

A set of mossy paving slabs led through the mist-wreathed garden. The slabs were made from crushed white sea shells so no matter how delicately the youngsters walked, a loud crunching sound betrayed their presence. And no escaping child wants to reveal their presence, especially not on Halloween.

Cuthbert and Fatima hoped so much that Mrs Hubbard would be home. She was their port in a storm, their lifeboat, their lighthouse shining bright.

"What if she doesn't live here any more?" asked Fatima, suddenly. "She was very old."

Cuthbert hesitated. There was no more colour to drain from his milky white face, but his shoulders slumped in disappointment and his eyes began to fill. Fatima wished she hadn't spoken. She reached boldly up and pulled a frayed bell-rope which was dangling from the roof of the porch. It rang once, rather gloomily. DONG!

All was dampness and fog.

An eternity seemed to pass while they waited, Cuthbert and Fatima, with their big eyes and gangling limbs and hopeful, fastbeating hearts.

"Please let her be in," Fatima repeated to herself over and over. "Please let her be kind."

Fatima pulled the rope a second time.

"She's not at home," Cuthbert sighed, already resigned to the worst.

But then came the sound of steps from within. They began from a long way off, taking for ever to arrive. The door, paint faded almost back to the original wood, opened slowly, and there before them stood a tiny but familiar figure.

"Well bless my cotton-pickin' tootsies! My sweety-pies! What ever did take you children so long?"

Cuthbert and Fatima looked at each other in surprise. Had Mrs Hubbard really been expecting them?

"Come in, come in!" she continued, thinking, in her befuddled way, that they were the children from the local school come for their party, and quite forgetting their original meeting.

The house smelled warm and welcoming after the dankness of the garden. For a moment it was almost too much for the Gruesome Twosome. They hovered on the step, like nervous birds.

Mrs Hubbard turned and smiled. "And I think your masks are very fine!"

"We're not wearing masks," replied Fatima, a little wearily.

Oliver the cat emitted a sour purr. These odd callers reminded him of a couple of skinny pigeons. He licked his lips.

Finally a faint glow of recognition stole into the old lady's eyes. "I seem to know you two kiddytots from somewhere . . . though I don't know where, and I don't know when. . ." She attempted to cast her mind back. "Were you with us last year, on the white water rafting expedition?"

Fatima quickly decided the real story of their meeting might be too long and confusing.

"No," she replied, "but this is not the first time our paths have crossed."

Mrs Hubbard's home had a long hallway, decorated with photographs of explosions through the ages. There were rooms leading off it in all directions. Fatima and Cuthbert had never seen such a grand place.

"This way, my pretties," hummed Mrs H. "This way to the kitchen!"

On one side, Fatima saw a magnificent staircase, carpeted with rich, red velvet. And above that, a chandelier, one of the grandest in the world, made by Monsieur Phillipe of France.

Cuthbert could smell food.

"I reckon I was expecting a bigger crowd," continued Mrs Hubbard in her high, quivering voice. "Perhaps more of you little folk will be along later?"

Fatima smiled, confused. A vague fear whispered to her that Mrs Hubbard had somehow invited the rest of the circus, but she pushed the thought away.

"My what odd little fiddlypops you are!" beamed the old lady when she could finally see them by the lights of the kitchen. "Home grown, clean cut, and neat as ninepence! But isn't it a little late to be out and about without any shoes?"

Cuthbert tried in vain to cover his mud-spattered feet. They'd lost their Indian moccasins during their week-long trek to Windflower.

"Never mind, you'll soon warm up by the fire."

Fatima's cheeks were already glowing as they hadn't glowed in years.

"Allow me take your cloaks. My, what lovely costumes! Aren't they lovely, Oliver?"

Oliver the cat pulled an extra sour face.

"Oh, don't mind him," smiled the old lady, "he gets a little jealous now and then."

Cuthbert, Fatima and Oliver eyed each other uneasily. Cuthbert had suffered some bad experiences whilst feeding the big cats in the circus. His tiny hands still bore the scratches and scars.

Fatima tugged her brother closer and whispered into his ear. "Don't start any arguments, Cuthbert. This is a new start for us. We all have to get along together!"

Cuthbert raised an eyebrow and then nodded. He bent down to the ginger tom and began to stroke it.

"Let us be good neighbours my feline friend."

Oliver blinked slowly and slunk off to another room.

Mrs Hubbard was looking up at a clock on the wall, the hands of which appeared to be made from sticks of dynamite. "I can't think what has happened to the rest of your classmates. Miss Palermo is normally so reliable. What could have kept her?"

Cuthbert and Fatima shrugged their frail shoulders. They didn't know who Miss Palermo was, and they had no knowledge of why she'd not shown up. But in their minds they could only imagine one person who might have detained her this fogbound and frightening Halloween night . . . it was a name they never wanted to hear of again. Finian Macabre!

CHAPTER THIRTY-THREE

Macabre Alone

FOGHORN TRUMPETER
HOPE FADES!

The anniversary of the disappearance of tiny twins Cuthbert and Fatima O'Hanlon passed quietly yesterday. Police say hopes of finding the missing babes are fading fast as they will now almost be toddlers.

Macabre sat alone in his monkey-skin chair, amidst the smell of cheap perfume and popcorn, reading the letter from the Maharajah of Rhajibangaloor. He read it over and over again, imagining afresh the scene when the circus arrived: crowds and kiddytots, sultans and elephants, diamonds and jewels. . .

"This is what we have waited for all these dark years. The chance to make it the best, like it was in the old days."

On the walls of his carriage, old posters looked down, faded as yellow as his teeth: the great performers of a hundred years ago; "Boldini the Clown", "Cheechee the Mind Reading Chimpanzee",

125

"Françoise and Family, Kings of the High Trapeze". A time when the Circus Macabre was the greatest circus of them all. Impossible to get hold of a ticket in those days. Queues from Allahmabama to Zambuktoo.

Macabre's eye came to light on a picture of the Gruesome Twosome. It had been taken when they were babies, and showed them practising on a trampoline.

Palefrightened faces looking out at the camera.

"And you," snarled Macabre at their image, "you two will not spoil this for me. If His Excellency wants to see you throw knives then he SHALL!" Macabre stared at the photograph so intensely that the glass within the frame cracked like ice. The picture of Cuthbert and Fatima floated down towards the toffee-apple-sticky carpet and lay there, face down, whilst the ringmaster's evil laugh filled not only his own carriage but the entire length of the train.

CHAPTER THIRTY-FOUR

Airborne

Badhagg's flight took her west across the town. From time to time she spoke into a small receiver strapped to her wrist.

"Badhagg to Ringmaster – Badhagg to Ringmaster – Do you read me? Over. . ."

A crackle of electricity and then the sound of Macabre's reply, loud and impatient, "Read you?! Why would I want to read you? What are you? A book?! Where are the Gruesome Twosome? Out!"

The witch and her broom swooped down past the statue of J T Doodlebug, dynamite tycoon, almost knocking off part of his moustache.

Macabre was still haranguing her via the receiver. "Our boat sails tomorrow, the riches of the Orient await us. Don't let me down!"

Badhagg switched off communications. She was so angry with the ringmaster's endless demands, she lost control of her broom for a moment. A brief passage through a storm cloud sent her plummeting rapidly down, down, down towards misty moors and fields and graveyards. . .

During her descent her mind strayed to the bond that bound her to Macabre. And as the crone's mind began to race she turned over in her mind the events of the past years, whilst at the same time counting down to the time when she would be free of the top-hatted tyrant for ever. That moment was fast approaching. Like the ground beneath the witch's broom. . .

She careered through a spiny-fingered elm tree, emerging with a startled owl on the end of her broom.

"Sorry, no hitch-hikers!" Badhagg hissed. With a flourish of her fingers, the luckless bird vanished in a puff of white smoke.

The momentary loss of control had accidentally sent Badhagg's broom spinning in the direction of Gravestone Walk. The same Gravestone Walk where Mrs Hubbard resided and was at that very moment serving gingerbread men to Cuthbert and Fatima.

A chill night breeze ruffled the witch's cloak. For a moment she was part of the ink-black sky itself.

"A little toad tells me I'm getting very close," she intoned to herself.

As if on cue, a toad emerged from the sleeve of her dress and gave a loud and disgusting belch. "You're very close."

"Thank you, Prince Eugene," replied Badhagg, with a laugh like shards of glass. "I think the Gruesome Twosome's luck has just run out!"

CHAPTER THIRTY-FIVE

Zombies

*L*isa left the safety of her car and crept into the fairground.

Inside, an eerie merry-go-round melody filled the air. There were lots of people walking aimlessly around, young and old alike, their faces all wearing the same blank expressions. From out of the corner of her eye, Lisa glimpsed her good friend, Les, from the corner store. Surely he would know something. She called out to him: "Hey! Les!"

Les didn't answer. He didn't even stop walking, he just carried on right past her. "I love to ride the fairground rides," he droned. "Big Dipper. Wheel of Death. I must try them all. . ."

Lisa reached out. "Les – it's me – Lisa!"

But Les had vanished into the mist, heading towards the Helter-Skelter. Lisa soon noticed another familiar face. A small child, eating a toffee apple.

"Sadie! Sadie Finkle!"

Sadie was one of Lisa's favourite and brightest pupils. It was she who'd painted the beautiful diorama of the fairground for parents' night.

"Thank goodness, Sadie. What's happening here?"

Sadie looked up and Lisa's hopes were dashed in the same instant. Sadie's eyes were as dim as the distant sea.

"It's the greatest show on earth," she began in a voice which barely seemed her own. "Ghost trains, bearded ladies, and all the toffee apples you can eat. . ."

For a second Lisa lost patience. She shouted at Sadie, grabbing her angrily by the shoulders. "Wake up, you silly girl! What's going on here? Why are you all behaving like this? Who did this to you?"

Sadie smiled again as though she hadn't heard a word. "It's the greatest show on earth."

Blank eyes. Everyone with blank eyes. And so her kids hadn't escaped after all. They must all be here somewhere, trapped in this spooky sideshow.

Lisa's gaze followed Sadie as she walked off. Past a huge man in a leopardskin, blowing fire by the main gate. She couldn't stop staring because the man seemed to have two heads. A jet of flame leapt high into the chill night air, and then from the second head, more flames. A clown on a unicycle drew up next to Fire-and-Brimstone and the two (or three of them, depending how you looked at it) began talking in whispers. From time to time they glanced across at Lisa.

Lisa felt very afraid again. Slowly, trying not to draw attention to herself, she walked away and attempted to mingle among the crowd. She even tried to make her face look as vacant as everyone else's. A shiver ran the length of her spine and left her heart all-a-thump.

I'm the only one who hasn't been turned into some kind of fairground zombie! she thought, in terror.

Lisa tried to keep the two-headed fire-eater in view. Where was he now? Was it just her imagination or was the back of her neck beginning to glow as warm as coals? To her right, the entrance to the fairground lay guarded by two penguins carrying spiked umbrellas. Lisa's head began to swim. *Don't panic, that's the worst thing you can do.*

A series of questions now flashed into Lisa's mind. How come she was the only person in the whole town not to have been affected? And where had this circus suddenly appeared from? Were they in any way linked to the strange events unfolding before her eyes?

A tricycling clown sped by, almost knocking her to the ground, whilst a chill gust of wind reminded her that the night was drawing in. Uncertain as to what to do next, without anyone to confide in, Lisa began to sink into a mood of dark despair.

I need to get out of here, she thought, searching for an exit. Looking around, Lisa found herself on a muddy strip of ground running behind a row of tents and stalls.

A high fence encircled the whole showground, but just where she stood was a gap where a couple of naughty schoolkids had kicked in the slats a couple of months back. Lisa figured that she could probably make it through.

"Roll up . . . roll up! The Big Wheel is about to turn!" boomed a voice from out of the gloom. Lisa was halfway through the hole in the fence when the end of her police jacket snagged on a large splinter.

"Shoot!" Lisa tugged and the piece of material tore off. She would owe Les a few buckeroos for that.

PARP! PARP! An old-fashioned horn sounded from behind her, and within seconds two clowns appeared, followed by Fire-and-Brimstone the fire-eater. Had something about her appearance alerted them to the fact that she wasn't under the hypnotic spell? A jet of flame suddenly hurtled in her direction by way of answer.

Lisa was through the gap in the fence and running. Uniform torn, legs shaking. Her legs hardly seemed to move at all. Where had she parked her car? It was difficult to see through the sea-fret and milling crowds. But difficult, too, for the pursuing circus army. Lisa spotted her motor and fumbled with the keys.

The key wouldn't go in the lock. She was shaking all over.

"Come on . . . come on!"

Clowns closing in on her.

Jets of fire.

Smell the paraffin smoke.

The key in the lock, turning.

Heartthump.

"Pl-eeeease start first time. . ."

CHAPTER THIRTY-SIX

Home Entertainment

Cuthbert, Fatima, and Mrs Hubbard were sitting in front of a large, roaring fire; Cuthbert thought he could see Macabre's face in the flames, leering out at him, but he tried to put this thought from his mind, and instead dunked a gingerbread man into his glass of hot milk. The head of the gingerbread man dissolved too quickly and fell to the bottom of the glass. Cuthbert took this to be a bad sign.

"Tonight is a night for fun and games," announced Mrs Hubbard, "if only your classmates would get here. I have all manner of tricks and treats to show you. Snakes and their ladders, hoola-the-hoop, hunt the thimbles."

Cuthbert looked up, a sudden darkness in his eyes. "I smell danger." What little colour there was had drained from his sunken cheeks.

"Yes, that's the spirit," replied Mrs Hubbard, thinking he was trying to get into the Halloween mood. "Tonight is the night for witches and ghouls!" She chuckled.

"So you can smell her too?" continued Cuthbert, somewhat surprised. Fatima gave her brother a sudden kick. But Mrs Hubbard thought the children were still fooling.

Fatima was now every bit as concerned as her brother, for she too could detect the witch's aroma.

"Badhagg!" she whispered to Cuthbert. "She must be close." Together brother and sister crossed to a dramatic, gothic window overlooking the garden.

A faint black line had just traced the skies overhead. It wouldn't have meant much to you or I but to the well-trained witch-watcher it was enough.

"It can only be her," continued Fatima, in a voice full of dread. "She never could fly a straight line."

And in that same instant the witch's senses had detected the nearby pitterpat of frightened hearts; her eyes, ravenblack and razorsharp, searched back and forth.

Cuthbert examined the sky for a second time but there wasn't much to be seen any more. The cloud was thick and the swirling fog blotted out what little light there was. "How close was she, do you think?"

"Too close," replied his sister, voice a-tremble.

CHAPTER THIRTY-SEVEN

Car Chase

The engine of Lisa's car continued to screech and squeal in protest.

"C'mon! C'mon!" she shouted in frustration. She spun the steering wheel and reversed backwards without even looking. Something clunked against the back bumper, but she didn't care. Anything to get away from the Circus Army.

Macabre's followers were still in hot pursuit, realizing that Badhagg's spell and the hypnotic umbrellas had somehow not caught Lisa in their net.

"After her!" shouted Mr Spangly, waving his arms wildly. "Let no one escape this place! Those are the chief's orders!"

In her rearview mirror Lisa saw Fire-and-Brimstone, the two-headed fire-eater looming close. And just behind him, the tattooed strongman and a couple of clowns with limegreen wigs. Lisa's car skidded a little, but she held on and accelerated away from the menacing circus folk.

Heartthump. Drythroat.

"Made it!" she gasped. Only now she wasn't alone. The evil clowns had bundled themselves into a battered dodgem car, and driven it out on to the road. Its overhead pole crackled ominously with sudden jolts of brightblue electrical charge. Lisa's trembling hands shifted her car into top gear . . . the engine growled like she'd never heard it growl before.

At first she had no idea where she was heading, her mind was jumbled. She'd seen some of her class at the fairground but what had happened to the coach party? She had to get to Mrs Hubbard's place and find out. If only she could shake those clowns off her tail. . . .

Lisa's driving wasn't very good at the best of times. She'd be the first to admit that but now the speed gauge was showing "eighty miles per hour". She couldn't remember having seen it read that before. And yet the dodgem car was still hot in pursuit. Closing in on her even. . .

Lisa did have one advantage though. She knew the streets of Windflower better than any clown.

Left into Shortfuse View. There was Les's store. Lights out, no one at home. Poor Les. Then right, hard right, past the statue, watch that kerb! Past the barber's shop and Harry's Fishing Supplies ("*Let Harry tackle it*"). . .

"Curses!" A glimpse of limegreen hair and a spark of blue in her rearview mirror told Lisa they were still right behind. Her foot was now flat down on the accelerator. The old car hadn't ever had to take this kind of treatment before. Not even when she'd lent it to her mum, who missed gears for a living.

The mist was closing in again. Lisa could see the railway crossing up ahead. The warning lights began to change.

"Come on!"

The clowns were still behind.

Engine groaning, Lisa's car sped through the barriers with seconds to spare. But she forgot to reduce speed as she hit the rails.

KERCHUNG!

There was a series of jolts as the car bounced up and down, struggling to make it over the railway lines, and the entire contents of her glove compartment spilled out on to the floor.

Lisa glanced in her mirror. The twin white barriers of the level crossing were down and a warning bell had begun to sound.

CLANG! CLANG!

The 19.21 goods train from Greed to Badapple began to roll by. And no matter how loudly the clowns hooted their horns, it continued to roll by. By the time the light finally turned green and the barrier rose slowly upwards, Lisa Palermo and her beat-up old motor had already vanished into the night. She was safe. At least for now. . .

CHAPTER THIRTY-EIGHT

ONE YEAR AGO...

WINDFLOWER GAZETTE

Today we welcome a new teacher to our local school. Lisa Pulermo. Lisa hails from faraway Shakespeer Bay, but has impressed us all with her enthusiasm and qualifications.

We at the Gazette join all our readers in wishing her evry success in raising the little Windflorians of the future.

How long ago all that seemed. Now Lisa's old Pontiac was pulled over at the bottom of Gravestone Walk with its engine steaming. She turned off the ignition and checked her mirrors to see if the street was as empty as it looked.

Everything was silent. At last a chance for her to gather her thoughts.

"Think straight, Lisa," she told herself. "Consider the facts and then go on from there." That's what she always told her kids when they were overexcited or worried about something.

Fact one, this wasn't a dream. If it had been she would have woken up screaming long ago. Fact two, the people of the town weren't behaving normally.

They looked like they'd been hypnotized or put under some kind of spell. Fact three, it was Halloween. Fact four, her kids were in trouble. Fact five, there was some weird circus in town and they had to have something to do with this. OK, so that wasn't a fact, maybe they were all the facts she knew for now, and the rest was just guesswork.

She herself hadn't been put under a spell like everyone else, and that was the only good news so far. Her next move was going to be to call on Mrs Hubbard to see if any of her class had made it there safely. But was that such a good move? Was there anyone left in this town she could trust?

Though the street looked deserted, the mist around the graveyard shifted and twisted itself into ghostly shapes until Lisa became convinced there must be someone out there, watching her. She turned off her headlights and wished this night was over. . .

CHAPTER THIRTY-NINE

Who's Out There?

DUM-DUM-DUM!

Mrs Hubbard heard the knock at the door and rose unsteadily to her feet. She still had very sharp hearing despite her advanced age and a lifetime's involvement with high explosives. At the same time, Cuthbert and Fatima had frozen like two of the white marbled statues in the nearby graveyard.

"Badhagg!"

"The witch always knocks thrice."

"Was that the door, children?" asked Mrs Hubbard, but only to make conversation, because she knew very well that someone had just knocked very boldly at her house. By the time she'd turned to Cuthbert and Fatima they had already vanished.

"Gone to hide from their schoolfriends, Oliver, that's what they've done, hehehe, they surely are a couple of scamps!"

Oliver blinked with quiet contempt as Mrs Hubbard shuffled off to open the door.

Cuthbert and Fatima, hearts a-flutter, had frantically searched for somewhere to conceal themselves, deciding eventually on a cupboard beneath the stairs. It was dark and cold and covered with cobwebs. Terrified though they were, the twins began sharpening their knives and preparing for a fight.

"We must battle for our freedom!" whispered Cuthbert.

"I'm with you, bro!"

"Cursed be he or she who first cries hold!"

"No surrender this time," nodded his sister.

In the distance they heard a second knock at Mrs Hubbard's door. It was so loud that for a moment they imagined someone was knocking at the door to their new hiding place beneath the stairs. Fatima held her brother's hand as they wondered what new disaster was about to befall them.

Lisa didn't intend knocking a third time. She guessed Mrs Hubbard might be getting a little deaf in her old age. Or what if she too had been hypnotized and was back at the fairground, enjoying the delights of the Waltzer or the Ghost Train?

Suddenly Lisa heard the sound of locks being unfettered.

CREAAAAAAK. . . The door opened so slowly Lisa could feel her heart knotting like twisted rope.

"Mrs Hubbard! Thank goodness!" she gasped, on seeing the frail old lady standing in front of her. "Are you OK?"

Mrs Hubbard didn't seem anything other than her usual cheerful, eccentric self. "Why, Miss Palermo," she hummed, taking Lisa by the hand. "We were expecting you some time ago, you naughty thing. But. . ."

She was looking over Lisa's shoulder, back into the garden. "But where are the rest of the children?"

Lisa's explanation trailed off even before it had begun. "I, er . . . don't really know what I can tell you. . ."

Mrs Hubbard ushered her into the porch, where they were met by the smell of hot coal, and warm ginger, and pampered cat.

"Why, Miss Palermo, I've only just noticed your costume. Well trickety-treat, how unusual . . . a police officer!"

Lisa wandered down the corridor, still in a daze. But it felt good to be inside this wonderful old house at last and comforting to find someone else not under the evil spell.

"I do have two of your children here," continued Mrs Hubbard. "My, what a couple of characters they are. Such wonderful costumes."

"Oh good," answered Lisa, with a vague feeling of unease she couldn't explain. "Which children do you have?"

Mrs Hubbard was looking around the hallway. "They were here a moment ago. I think they must be playing hide and seek."

"You don't remember their names?"

"I'm sorry, Miss Palermo, but they never did introduce themselves. I think we must get them to do so right now, don't you? Oh, children!" Mrs Hubbard called out in a high, sweet voice. "Children? Miss Palermo is here . . . do come and show her your fine costumes. . ."

Inside the darkened cupboard, Fatima and Cuthbert held their breath. They were used to doing this when Macabre was on the rampage, and they had become very good at it. Two minutes was their record. They could hear Mrs Hubbard talking about them but couldn't make out what she was saying. Cuthbert detected another voice in the hallway. A woman's voice. Young, he guessed. Certainly under a hundred. But as he strained to hear more, Cuthbert lost balance for a moment, grabbed at Fatima for support, missed, and fell hard against the cupboard door.

"Wooaaah!" With a loud crash young Cuthbert landed right at the feet of Mrs Hubbard and her visitor. When he glanced up, the first thing he saw was Lisa Palermo's look of amazement.

"Well *there* you are!" gasped old Mrs Hubbard. "We never would have found you."

The cobweb-strewn cupboard creaked again, and out from her hiding place stepped Fatima. She half hid herself behind the old wooden doll's house that had fallen out at the same time as her brother.

Cuthbert still held the knife in his hand.

"They would never have taken us alive!"

"We were ready to fight to the death."

"Aren't they priceless!" beamed Mrs Hubbard. "I can't wait for the Christmas show."

Lisa was looking puzzled. Even allowing for the masks and costumes, she was sure these two little waifs weren't from her class. "Children? What are your names? Can you take your masks off for a moment?"

"These aren't masks," answered Cuthbert, curtly. He liked the look of Lisa's face though. It was friend-lier than the ones he was used to seeing beneath the Big Top. No make-up. No wig. Kind eyes. Fatima was looking at the teacher too. Was this a face they could trust?

"I am Cuthbert," announced the older of the twosome, on the spur of the moment.

"And I am Fatima," rejoined his sister.

They both bowed with a deep flourish that might have been taken for sarcasm, though it wasn't meant like that.

"Are you brother and sister?" asked Mrs Hubbard.

"Two pillars hewn from the same rock," replied Cuthbert, which was his way of saying "yes".

Lisa Palermo, dressed like a cop, and now starting to act like one, still wanted to know more. She blew out her cheeks and eyed the two kids up and down for the umpteenth time. They sure were a couple of oddballs. Lisa had been a teacher for several years and taught lots of kids, but none of them remotely resembled the Gruesome Twosome: pale, with talcum-powder complexions, thin as string; dark, staring, neverblink eyes.

"Are you two from Miss Kernowitz's class?"

144

The twins shook their heads.

"We don't know who she is," replied Fatima in a thin, monotonous voice.

"Now please, children – what happened to the rest of your classmates? This is serious now, no more silly replies!" Lisa's patience was at an end. It had been a long day. But her flash of anger produced only silence from the Gruesome Twosome. They were used to staying tight-lipped when someone shouted at them.

Lisa tried softening her tone. "What is happening here? If you know anything you must tell me so I can help. Why is everyone behaving so oddly? I've just been down to the fairground and ended up being chased by a bunch of clowns trying to kill me!"

For Cuthbert and Fatima time seemed to stop. It was the final confirmation of what they'd most feared. Badhagg wasn't alone. Macabre and his circus were in town. And he wouldn't rest until they were back in his thrall.

They remained for a while with their heads bowed. Had their dream of freedom come to an end so soon? Two frightened, troubled souls. What now? Where to run? Who to trust? Fatima and Cuthbert exchanged a look. They glanced across at Lisa. Sometimes you have to believe in someone. . .

Fatima spoke first. "We are runaways from the Circus. They have come here to take us back."

Cuthbert nodded. "Badhagg the witch was outside a moment ago."

Lisa turned in fear, half expecting to see a pointyhatted crone striding towards her. Mrs Hubbard clapped her hands together delightedly, believing this was all part of the show, and went off to bake more cookies.

Lisa couldn't quite believe what she'd just heard. Witches. Circus runaways. It would have sounded completely absurd if she hadn't just been to the fairground and seen for herself. "Could this witch have put the town under a spell?" she asked.

Fatima shrugged her frail shoulders. "We don't know. We weren't there. But that would certainly be her style."

Lisa's eyes narrowed. Everything about their appearance and actions convinced her that these two little waifs were the key to the evening's weird turn of events. She laid an arm, gently, round the children's shoulders.

"Look, why don't you tell me the whole story, right from the beginning?"

CHAPTER FORTY

REPORT OF DEKE TRUBBLE,
GENERAL SECRETARY OF
THE FOGHORN FALLS UFO SOCIETY,
NOV. 2ND, 19--

Visibility was very poor this Halloween, but several sightings were reported by our members, with a specially high concentration of reports around the town and locality of Windflower. I myself witnessed a series of lightning flashes low over the sea, followed by the appearance of a cigar-like object, which then accelerated away at speed.

Sadly I must also mention a certain EX-member of the society (whose name I won't disclose) and who radioed me to say that she had sighted a witch, flying on a broom, and performing a series of aerial stunts. Members are reminded that this is a serious society, staffed by volunteers, and we do NOT have time to waste on childish pranks and crank observations.

* * *

An angry Macabre was watching the Big Wheel turn round and round. Still no news of the two escapees. And the clock was ticking down to the hour when the Maharajah's ship would set sail. Without the Gruesome Twosome he knew there would be no point in embarking. And after one week the runaways were still at liberty. Why was he surrounded by such fools?

Macabre's brow furrowed as he remembered how his mother had predicted disaster for the circus once he took over.

"You have a large head, son," she once told him, "but not one suited for business."

He wasn't about to see her proved right. No sir. Macabre's Circus would once again be the best show in the world, whether people liked it or not! The sight of Windflower's zombified townsfolk with no choice but to explore the various rides and attractions brought an ugly smile to the ringmaster's cracked lips.

While the Big Wheel carried on turning and the music played, sadmerrygoroundwaltzer, Macabre suddenly noticed a distant speck silhouetted against the faint, silvery moon.

"Badhagg . . . so she returns at last! Let us hope for her sake that she has some news of those irksome midgets!"

Mr Spangly, as ever, was reduced to tears at the thought of it all. "I'm sure she will have done her best," he sniffed, blowing his nose on to the piano-key lapels of his jacket.

"Her best?! She'll have to do better than that! What use is failure when there are hungry lions to feed? I want the Gruesome Twosome back here, ready for our trip to the East, and then, once I've found a better act to replace them, they can take a one-way trip on the Ghost Train!"

He laughed horribly, showing an excess of green, sharksharp teeth, with one silversparkle filling. His laughter grew louder and louder.

Badhagg herself, having completed a circuit of the fairground, was now making an easterly approach over the Big Wheel. "Badhagg to ground control," she hissed into her radio receiver. "Coming in to land."

Inside a small fairgound tent, a fierce-looking penguin was hunched over a large, glowing eyeball. "Air traffic control to Badhagg, you are cleared to land."

Sheriff Cohnberg was seated on the Ferris Wheel, holding a coconut which he'd somehow won, and a stick of candyfloss. The vacant, empty smile looked like it had been painted on to his face. Normally the most alert individual in town, he didn't even glance up as the straggly-haired, wild-eyed witch flew within a whisker of the seat in which he was sitting.

Badhagg made a smooth landing right in front of the Ghost Train. She pulled off her goggles and walked over to Macabre, swaggering with pride.

"Well?" asked the evil ringmaster.

"Well?" asked Mr Spangly, in tears.

"Well?" squawked a penguin, holding an umbrella.

"Well?" enquired the Bearded Lady.

"Well it looks like my spell worked a treat," screeched Badhagg. "The whole town is here!"

Macabre was tapping with his fingers, impatiently. "Except for the girl who escaped."

Badhagg's eyes darkened. "Mmmm. I don't see how that could have happened, unless . . . she mustn't have been born in Windflower. It was an oversight in the way I cast the spell. If you find her for me I can soon rectify that."

Macabre smiled condescendingly. "I hope so. I wouldn't want to think you were losing your touch."

Macabre enjoyed the witch's look of resentment. "And the Gruesome Twosome?" he hissed. "What about them?"

"Good news," snapped Badhagg. "I know where they're hiding."

Macabre's eyes glowed with a new intensity, bright as the firebox on the Carnival Train, bright as the flames blown by Fire-and-Brimstone. The fire-eater in question also laughed, and great jets of flame shot sulphuryellow upwards towards the heavens.

CHAPTER FORTY-ONE

An Unwelcome Caller

The big fire crackled. Shadows leaped higher and higher up peeling plaster walls. Cuthbert and Fatima were still telling their story to Lisa. Cuthbert had hold of his sister by her ankles and had just tapped her head three times on the floor. "Bang bang bang!" he shouted. "The evil Macabre fired his revolver in our direction—"

"But we were too quick!" interrupted Fatima, springing to her feet and somersaulting acrobatically around the huge flickershadow room by way of demonstration.

"But our brave escape was doomed to failure. He came after us with wild poodles and strongmen, and carried us back," said Cuthbert.

Fatima crouched low by the fire. "And that was the last time we tried to escape, until last week, when my arrow finally delivered us from slavery."

Lisa had never heard such a tale. She imagined these children held captive in a circus, fired from cannons, pursued through the countryside by wild animals and evil clowns. "Could any man really be so cruel as this Macabre?"

"He is crueller than the cruellest sea," answered Cuthbert.

He was such a frail little thing, this boy standing in front of her, Lisa wondered how he'd survived so long in that terrible place. "And what about the others in the circus?" continued Lisa. "Have they also suffered like you?"

Fatima's eyes began to fill with tears. She waited until she had recovered herself before answering. "They are all as frightened as we, but too frightened of Macabre to step out of line. We're for the flying trapeze if ever we're found – and no safety net!"

Mrs Hubbard entered the room, carrying chocolate ice cream in beautiful stickofdynamite-shaped glasses.

"Now then, you trick-or-treaters, isn't this fun? Have the rest of the class arrived yet?"

Cuthbert threw a glance at the window opposite. "May heaven help anyone out there tonight!"

"Oh they'll be fine," breezed Mrs Hubbard, pulling a set of thick, shabby velvet curtains across the window. "It's a fine evening and the fog will lift as soon as the tide goes out."

Cuthbert continued to stare through a chink in the curtains. "The witch, Badhagg, knows our whereabouts. She'll call again before the night is through. And this time Macabre and the others will be with her."

Lisa was concerned to see the Gruesome Twosome so frightened. She had never seen fear like that in kids so young. "So you think this witch already knows where you are?"

Fatima nodded.

"We have to flee," stammered Cuthbert. "Lead us to the hills and fields!"

"But you haven't finished your ice cream," interjected old Mrs Hubbard, handing Cuthbert a spoon.

Cuthbert looked puzzled. "I scream?"

"So what's to stop the witch casting a spell on us now? Turning us into zombies like the rest of the town?" persisted Lisa.

"We know her magic," replied Fatima, "her spells only work on the unwary. Once you know that voice you know never to listen to anything it says."

"You have been warned," muttered Cuthbert, ominously.

Satisfied with the reply, Lisa was just about to sit down at a little table next to rows of pies and pumpkins and pastries, when she happened to glance up towards the window. What she saw there caused her to drop her own spoon with a loud clatter. Through the chink in the curtains she could see the silhouette of a clown's head!

CHAPTER FORTY-TWO

A postcard sent by Emilia Bronti to her sister,
Charlottina. October --, 19--:

Dear Charlottina,

Windflower really is the most horrid place. Albert and I arrived here, on the night of Halloween, a festival practised with great enthusiasm by the locals. And what an odd crowd they are!

On our visit to a nearby fairground, which was very busy, everyone was going about their business as though they were zombies! Believe it! Not one person spoke to us during the whole period of our visit to the town from the moment we arrived to the moment we left. Not an ounce of hospitality. I assure you we won't be listening to any of your recommendations again.

Your loving but dismayed sister,

Emilia

***

"Get down you fool!" hissed Macabre through scissorsharp teeth. "They'll see you!"

An orange-haired clown with a brightpainted smile drew in his long jack-in-the-box neck and began to cry.

"I'm s-s-sorry . . . I didn't mean to get it wrong!"

Mopping his tears, which had made his make-up run grotesquely, the clown retreated to the ranks.

There, a double row of ringside wrong-doers stood cowering before their black-cloaked chief. There were clowns, moth-eaten wild beasts, snarling poodles in spangled costumes, penguins. . .

Macabre turned and addressed them all in a low, threatening voice. "From now on there must be no mistakes!"

The orange-haired clown began sobbing again.

"Our attack will be swift and decisive. They won't know what has hit them!"

His followers nodded as one.

"They might think they're safe, hiding like rats in their dank little hole –" Macabre turned and looked up at Mrs Hubbard's house – "but it won't do them any good. By the time this hour is out they'll be back with us . . . where they belong!"

Inside that same crumbling, under-siege homestead, Cuthbert and Fatima had indeed decided to hide. Lisa was trying hard to dissuade them, but learning, too, how determined these strange little waifs could be.

155

"I'll look after you," she promised Fatima. "And Mrs Hubbard is here. We've locked all the windows and doors. I don't see how anyone could get in."

Fatima didn't answer but crossed to a large unlit chimney on the far side of the room. Cuthbert was already standing in the hearth with a bag over his shoulder.

"Fatima? What kind of creatures live in the chimneys of old houses?"

"All creatures, great and small," replied his sister, knowledgeably. "Bats, racoons, spiders and owls. There are some that flaps and some that prowls."

Fatima began to climb up the chimney.

"Er, I don't think you should do that," interrupted Lisa, when she saw what they were planning. "Isn't the chimney a little narrow? It – it'll be dangerous. . ."

Lisa could hear Fatima's voice, now muffled, and growing fainter.

"Don't worry about us. We know how to look after ourselves. . ."

Cuthbert had now vanished from view too.

"Will there really be bats?" wobbled his voice in the gloom.

"No . . . hopefully not," answered Fatima, ever more faintly.

Silence. Windhowl. Batflap.

Lisa was peering up the chimney. There was already no sign of the Gruesome Twosome. Just a smell of soot and coal.

Mrs Hubbard's eyes twinkled faintly. "Are the

children unhappy?" she enquired, having just arrived holding a plate heaped high with steaming mince pies.

"No. No of course not," answered Lisa, not sure how much detail she should reveal. "I think they're really happy here but there is something in this neighbourhood that has terrified them. Someone is after them. . ."

"Poor little souls." Mrs Hubbard's lips turned down a little, with concern. "We must do something about that, Miss Palermo. I'll not have my kiddypops living in fear!"

And when Lisa looked she saw that a fierce resolve had crept into those fadedsnowflakeeyes.

Lisa and Mrs Hubbard stared back up the flue.

"Cuthbert? Fatima? Are you two OK?"

"Fine," came a distant reply.

"And dandy. . ." added a second echoing voice.

Lisa felt relieved. A teacher never likes to lose too many children in one day, especially not on Halloween.

THUD THUD THUD!

A sudden knock on the door interrupted Lisa's thoughts. This was no ordinary knock. It seemed to shake the old house to its very core. Things shook. Things rattled. Ornaments slid off shelves and chandeliers swayed from side to side.

A second knock. Even more forbidding than the first.

"Don't answer that!" shouted Cuthbert and Fatima, hidden together in the darkened chimney.

"Don't answer that!" shouted Lisa, from the sooty fireside hearth.

But Mrs Hubbard was already shuffling her way to the door, unfastening locks and turning rusted keys. "It must be the rest of the children, come at last for cookies and fun!"

CHAPTER FORTY-THREE

That's Entertainment

Clownes be happy
Clownes be sad
Clownes be good
But clowneth never for bad

(Taken from a 12th century manuscript,
"The arte of being a Clowne")

Mrs Hubbard slid open the final lock, unaware of the shouted warnings issuing forth from chimney and hearth.

Before her, framed against a cold, misty sky, stood a clown. A clown of sinister appearance with deathly white face, fiercepainted eyebrows, and a cruel, faintly ridiculous smile.

Mrs Hubbard clapped her hands together in delight. "Ah. At last! The children's en-ter-tain-er!"

The clown tooted his horn obligingly and began cycling round on a silver unicycle. The tune he played wasn't really a tune at all, it was more an out-of-tune, but Mrs Hubbard didn't mind. Ever since she was a little girl, she had loved the circus. She was so entranced by the performance that she failed to notice Fire-and-Brimstone slip past her and into the hallway.

Luckily Lisa wasn't quite so preoccupied. Fire-and-Brimstone had only got a few paces into the hall when he was struck over both heads with a silver cookie tray. The huge hairy fire-eater staggered first to one side, knocking a portrait in oils of Darius T Gelegnite to the ground en route, then to the other, where he collided with the wall. Lisa seized her opportunity and grabbed Mrs Hubbard firmly from behind. As Fire-and-Brimstone continued to stumble she added a second blow, on his bottom, which sent him sprawling out into the garden via a set of rickety timber steps.

In a flash the door was locked once more. Bolts drawn tight shut.

"Don't you like clowns, my dear?" asked Mrs Hubbard, still in a daze.

"Not when they are here to kidnap little children." And Lisa proceeded to tell the whole story of Cuthbert and Fatima and their escape from the circus. And as she was telling the story she continued checking and double-checking every catch on every window.

Mrs Hubbard was stunned to hear about Macabre's circus and their foul deeds. She kept shaking her snowy white head in disbelief.

Cuthbert and his sister remained jammed up the chimney, like a couple of frightened racoons. They knew in their tiny hearts that Macabre was still close, so close they could almost feel his angry stare upon them.

CHAPTER FORTY-FOUR

Spells, Plans, and Trouble in Store...

Outside 22a Gravestone Walk, Fire-and-Brimstone was rubbing his heads. Macabre had just added another clout of his own, even harder than Lisa's.

"Did you see the Gruesome Twosome?" snarled the top-hatted tyrant, his moustache twirling hysterically.

Fire-and-Brimstone shook his sore heads. "No, sir."

Badhagg had now joined them. "They must have been hiding, they must have been dodging. That's what they're good at after all."

Badhagg began enthusiastically chanting a spell.

Hubble Bubble
Toil and Trouble
Turn this house to
Dust and...

Macabre cut her off. "Not yet! Not yet! We've got to get those two runaways out first! They're too valuable

161

to vanish in a pile of rubble. We need them to entertain the Maharajah, remember?"

"Well that's easy enough then," smiled the crone in black. "Just send in the clowns."

Macabre nodded, apparently pleased at the suggestion. A whole row of silvery and sinister clowns tooted their horns to show they were ready.

"Don't give *me* orders!" snapped Macabre, his mood changing as suddenly as a set of railway points. "This is *my* evil plan and *I'll* think of what to do next! Right?"

Badhagg muttered under her breath but had the good sense to nod her head. No point in confronting that top-hatted tyrant just yet. Like any witch, she knew how to bide her time. And that time was fast approaching. Meanwhile Macabre had strode off into the mist to consult his penguin generals.

Mr Spangly watched as his chief strode by. A foolish thought now entered his head. He looked up at the chimney on Mrs Hubbard's house and saw a way to get in unobserved. He thought of how pleased Macabre would be with whoever could capture those troublesome kids. A joyous but evil smile ran the length of Mr Spangly's make-up as he crept towards a drainpipe covered in twirling ivy. . .

A wind, like children crying, blew down the flue of the chimney as Fatima saw a chink of light through the bricked-in gloom.

The chimney gave out on to the fireplace of a tiny

attic room at the very top of the house. Fatima's original plan had been to hide there until Macabre grew tired of searching for them, but she quickly realized that not even the Gruesome Twosome could spend their whole lives hiding up a chimney.

With a shower of dust and soot, and a thud of brick and plaster, the Gruesome Twosome emerged into Mrs Hubbard's attic. It was empty, except for a tattered circus poster on the wall, and an old rocking horse nodding away in a dark corner.

Cuthbert stroked the rocking horse, felt its long shabby mane made from knotted wool. "Whither would you carry us, my fine steed? Where will your speedy, silvery hooves lead us this night?" There was no light in the room – for the window pane hadn't been cleaned in an eternity – just a flicker from the foot of the chimney. Fatima was staring at it when she saw a little puff of dust emerge. Cuthbert saw it too. Brother and sister froze.

Another, bigger, cloud of dust and soot followed. Fatima held Cuthbert's hand, as they backed away, instinctively, towards the opposite wall.

At the base of the chimney there now stood a pair of feet. Giant feet. Not many of the good citizens of Windflower had feet that size. Joshua Jackson, the blacksmith, took a size thirteen. Edward Fingerman, the organist, a fourteen, but even their shoes would have been dwarfed by the bright red lace-ups now staring Fatima in the face. There was no doubt in her mind. These were clown's shoes!

"Mr Spangly!" she cried, looking round the room for any means of escape. There was none!

Mr Spangly, bent almost in two, was slowly emerging from the chimney, eyes glistening with wicked intent. His revolving bow-tie spun. He held a small bicycle horn in one hand.

TOOT!

Mr Spangly extended a very long arm in Cuthbert's direction. Cuthbert couldn't move. His legs shook like jelly. A cold white hand now rested on his trembling shoulders.

Fatima willed herself into action. She reached into Cuthbert's bag and produced a set of gleaming knives. There was a flash of silver and steel, followed by a timbery thud. She had pinned Mr Spangly's massive shoes in place with her twin blades. The evil clown began crying, though his face was filled with anger. It seemed no amount of struggling was going to free him or his giant red shoes.

Cuthbert and Fatima, tiny hearts pounding, searched the room in desperation for any sign of an exit. They couldn't use the chimney, for what if there were more clowns concealed there? The window led nowhere.

"There must be a door," stammered Fatima.

Mr Spangly was sounding his horn angrily. It sounded like a distress call.

TOOT! TOOT! TOOOOO-T!

His bow-tie whirred round in circles.

"Cuthbert!" gasped Fatima. She was crouched low

by a tiny locked door. Fatima's nimble fingers and the fine tip of the knife somehow conjured a promising "click" from the lock. The door swung open with a rusty, timeworn creak. "Let's go!"

TOOT! TOOT! TOOT! protested Mr Spangly's horn.

Cuthbert seemed reluctant to step out into the darkness. "'What if there are more clowns out there?"

Fatima wasn't listening. She locked the door behind them and led her brother on towards the gloomy stairwell. In the distance they could still hear the angry honk of Mr Spangly's horn.

"We have to go back downstairs," announced Fatima. "I think we need to trust Lisa and Mrs Hubbard to help us in our fight. I mean really trust them. Not run off at the first opportunity."

Cuthbert looked thoughtful. Their whole act was based on trust. Without it their routine would have fallen apart. But now they had to trust someone else. It was like stepping out on to a very long and wobbly tightrope. And tonight – Halloween night – there was no safety net!

"Then let us rejoin them," muttered Cuthbert, his mind only half made up and still sounding less than certain.

Rather than walk, the Gruesome Twosome slid down the banister, speeding past darkened, dusty floors, past statues and portraits of famous experts and pioneers from the world of explosives, past ancient potted plants and faded drapes.

And when they reached the main hallway, there to greet them stood Lisa and Mrs Hubbard, their faces etched with relief.

CHAPTER FORTY-FIVE

FATIMA'S DIARY

...Before we met Lisa and Mrs Hubbard we had never met a single kind person. Mrs Hubbard we had seen that day, long ago, fluffy clouds ago, when she gave us milk and cookies. And she had always stayed in our minds since then. She is an old lady but her eyes shine bright.

Lisa is a teacher she is twenty-five. I wish my hair was fine and dark like hers. She is tall but not like a clown on stilts. I like her eyes too, because they shine like sequins, or like precious jewels. I think Lisa and Mrs H will help us. Help us to face what is to come...

CHAPTER FORTY-SIX

Spangly and Bright

"They won't take this place easily," said Lisa, fixing the Gruesome Twosome with a determined gaze and hoping she could somehow make them feel safe even if they weren't. She drew the curtains back and peered out. "But first we gotta make sure all the chimneys are blocked up. You've just proved someone can get around the house that way. Cuthbert? Can you check the basement? Fatima, this floor – I'll take the upstairs rooms."

"I can help too," interjected Mrs Hubbard, keen to help out.

Before anyone could protest, before Cuthbert and Fatima could tell her about Mr Spangly still locked in the attic, the old dear had hurried off. For a woman of her advanced years she really was remarkable.

"Sto-p!" shouted Cuthbert and Fatima as one. They spluttered out the news to Lisa about Mr Spangly, newly arrived via the chimney.

"Mr Spangly?"

"He's very dangerous," explained Fatima, with widening eyes.

Cuthbert's face wore a worried frown. "He's the clown who put the slap in slapstick!"

Lisa ran to the stairs. "Quick! Cuthbert, you come with me. Fatima, look after things here!"

Cuthbert and Fatima looked at each other, then at Lisa, and then at the ground. It was only now that Lisa realized they couldn't bear to be separated. In fact they had *never* been separated.

Lisa grabbed Fatima's hand. "Come on then, we'll do this together!"

Meanwhile, in the damp and darkened attic above them, Mr Spangly had finally managed to free his giant shoes from the floor. He began rattling the door. From time to time he would give it an angry kick. His mood was growing darker and darker.

Mrs Hubbard, arriving on the other side of the same door, could see the lock rattling, apparently of its own accord. "Who's that?" she asked.

Mr Spangly's horn hooted by way of reply. An innocent, cunning, toot. But Mrs Hubbard was on her guard this time.

"Are you a clown? One of the naughty ones?"

A second, rather sad toot sounded back.

"What's that? You're sorry?"

A single duck-like toot. The saddest yet.

Mrs Hubbard's heart, soft as marzipan, was beginning to melt. "If I let you out, do you promise to be good?"

Mr Spangly's horn sounded a cheerful double note.

The old lady seemed satisfied and reached into her pocket for a set of spare keys.

With a huffing and a puffing, Lisa, Cuthbert and Fatima arrived on the top floor landing. Everything happening now in slow motion. . . .

"Don't open the door!" they yelled.

The key turned in the lock. . . .

The clown smiled. . . .

Too late! The door was already open, revealing Mr Spangly, red-eyed and dishevelled and full of dark intent. He took off his cone-shaped hat and smiled a grin of pure iniquity. Without a second's hesitation, he seized Mrs Hubbard around the waist and threw her over his shoulder.

"Hey!" shouted Lisa, angrily. "Put her down!"

Mr Spangly sprang back into the attic with his hostage.

Suddenly Cuthbert noticed the floorboard on which Mr Spangly was standing. The nail in it had just loosened, causing the wood to lift by a couple of milli-inches. The Gruesome Twosome had worked in circuses long enough to know the principles of leverage. They knew how a plank could be used to comic or acrobatic effect according to the force placed at either end: simple circus physics.

Cuthbert seized the moment and leapt forward, landing with a somersault and a thud on one end of the loose floorboard. His body may have been light but his timing was the best.

BEEEYOIIIIINGGG!

Mr Spangly was catapulted up into the air, causing him to release Mrs Hubbard from his grip. She too flew upwards, but in the opposite direction, performing one perfect mid-air rotation before being safely caught by a combination of Fatima and Lisa.

"Ayeooop!"cried Fatima, for old times' sake.

It would have been a 5.9 in any gymnastic contest.

Mr Spangly, meanwhile, had crashed through the window pane of the attic and was speeding through the night air in the opposite direction, screaming as he went. "Aaaaaaargh!"

In the garden beneath him, a circus rescue team quickly emerged and was soon trying to manoeuvre a large canvas sheet.

"Left a little!" shouted Macabre.

Confused, Olga the Bearded Lady (who didn't know her left from her right), took a step in the wrong direction. Mr Spangly fell straight past the outstretched sheet, and his fall was broken instead by a group of penguins. They collapsed in a heap like shinyblackninepins.

"Idiots!" raged Macabre. "And as for you," he yelled to Mr Spangly. "I'll teach you to act without waiting for orders!"

Mr Spangly, shaken, sore, and sobbing, knew that he was in for a terrible dressing-down.

CHAPTER FORTY-SEVEN

*B*arrabas had been dreaming of his children. The gentle rocking motion of the local train sent him quickly to sleep. A straggly beard had formed during the long months of his search and wisps of grey stolen into his hair. But he looked peaceful now, his head cradled on his kitbag, breathing softly. The gentle clatter of the rails acted as a lullaby to his tormented soul. And in his dreams, as always, were Cuthbert and Fatima. Their faces turned away from him – for how could he imagine their appearance with nothing but two faded portraits to go on?

A jolt woke the dozing lighthouse keeper from his slumbers. The train was slowing and a barely-lit station sliding into view. He wiped the sleep from his eyes and fastened his coat ready to face the night.

Barrabas O'Hanlon, lighthouse keeper, stood on the platform as the train pulled away, the faint glow of its lights clattering softly off into the distance.

How he had missed the sea, the swirling fogs, the tides battering against the door of his lighthouse, and the peaceful pulse of the great light flashing slowly offonoffon in the gloom. But he missed his missing babies even more. Cuthbert and Fatima. Where were they now, those ten-year-old babies? Who bought their candy, who combed their hair and helped them tie their tiny shoes?

"Windflower", read a quaint sign on the station wall. The platform itself was deserted, an icy wind blowing off the sea. Barrabas pulled up the collar of his jacket and wondered in which direction the town lay. He scanned the horizon for tell-tale lights but all he could see was the moon flitting from cloud to wind-driven cloud and the distant silhouette of a great wooden roller-coaster ride.

"That is the sort of place where candyfloss and apples would be sold," thought the lighthouse keeper, "and where clowns might gather."

A lean dog with dark, sorrowful eyes, a skinny frame and a wet muzzle angled up to the lighthouse keeper and more or less forced its head into the side of his leg.

"Ahoy there, boy – what you after, eh?"

The dog gazed up at Barrabas and licked his hand.

"What a very black dog. I don't think I've ever seen such a black dog before."

He felt the mongrel's collar for a name tag but there was nothing, just a sore spot where the collar had rubbed.

"'Blackdog' it will have to be then. Come on, old boy, no sense in us waiting round here." Slinging his bag over his shoulder, Barrabas leaned into the wind and headed off in the direction of the roller-coaster, followed, after a pause, by his new companion, Blackdog. It looked a long walk, but he felt hopeful of what they would find there, and made swift progress through the deserted suburbs.

CHAPTER FORTY-EIGHT

Council of War

In a fog-strewn garden, just beyond the graveyard, Macabre had summoned his closest advisers to a council of war. (All except for Mr Spangly, who was busy cleaning out the poodles' cages as part of his punishment.)

The vile ringmaster paced agitatedly in the shadow of the Carnival Train, parked in the shadow of the old yew tree.

He waved forward one of his penguin generals. "Are the troops ready?"

The penguin nodded.

Macabre's eyes were glowing like red-hot coals. "Then order the clowns forward!"

A chill wind blew frostfrozen leaves across gardens. Beneath the cover of the mist and darkness, Macabre's army stole in for the attack.

CHAPTER FORTY-NINE

Mrs Hubbard's house was a regular hive of activity. (Except for Oliver the cat, that is. He was watching events with his usual look of bored contempt.)

Cuthbert and Fatima were daubing their faces with a traditional Apache warpaint given to them by Sinking Bull, a real Indian Chief who had worked alongside them in the circus (until his request for a wage increase led to an unfortunate demise on the high trapeze).

Lisa removed a Zulu war shield from a panelled wall in the hall, and then armed herself with a matching spear. Mrs Hubbard was busy pouring gunpowder into an old blunderbuss. In her younger days, apparently, she had been quite a crack shot.

Cuthbert and Fatima started to set traps beneath windows and doors. Lisa was amazed how much they seemed to know about explosives and booby traps. Had she really led such a sheltered life? Mrs Hubbard was carefully positioning a pair of roller skates beneath the kitchen window. Cuthbert removed two large floorboards and then covered the hole with a rug.

From outside of the house there came an unexpected sound: it was the squeak of a rusty unicycle.

Out of the mist rolled a bowler-hatted clown, carrying a car horn, beneath which dangled a bedraggled white flag. He cycled to within a few feet of Mrs Hubbard's porch and then stopped, still wobbling perceptibly.

"Will you parley?" he called up to the windows of the house.

There was a pause before Cuthbert's face appeared at an upstairs window. "*Parlez-vous Français?*" he shouted down.

"*Non,*" replied the clown.

Lisa then appeared at a different window. "What are your terms?"

The clown unfurled a long sheet of parchment. "Surrender the Gruesome Twosome and the circus will leave town. The lives of your citizens will be returned to normal."

Fatima felt frightened. What if Lisa agreed? What were their small and insignificant lives when weighed against those of a whole town? Those of the children in Lisa's class? Her heartbeat skipped out of control. Silence hung over the great house and its garden. Fatima looked round to see Lisa standing next to her. The teacher gave her hand a reassuring squeeze. Her hands were warm. Fatima had never felt warm hands before.

Lisa crossed to the window and shouted down. "The kids stay here. Now go away, you're wasting your time!"

The bowler-hatted clown's expression turned

quickly to anger and he reached for a weapon concealed beneath his checked suit. Cuthbert saw his move: the bow drawn, arrow ready, a steady aim.

THWANG!

A sucker-tipped arrow sped, lightningfast, on to the clown's forehead, landing there with a resounding and satisfying THWUMP!

For an instant a deathly calm held sway. Even the frogs and crickets held their breath.

"ATTACK!" bellowed Macabre, waving his top hat frantically. "Send in the poodles!"

Poodles are normally thought of as friendly creatures. But anyone who'd seen Madame Mimi's circus act knew that this wasn't always the case. They were a savage bunch. Specially bred. Larger than average, though still possessing the same elaborate clipped coats and fancy tails as the rest of their breed. But there the resemblance ended. Madame Mimi's poodles had razorsharp fangs, untrimmed claws, and attitude to match. At Macabre's signal they began yapping ferociously, and propelled themselves forwards towards the house, balanced on flaming beach balls. Hot dogs!

Macabre laughed at the spectacle, revealing his dismal dentistry for all to see.

The poodles rolled closer and closer until, at the last moment, they leapt from the beach balls, leaving the flaming projectiles to career on in the direction of Mrs Hubbard's home.

"Goodness gracious, great balls of fire!" cried Mrs Hubbard in alarm.

Macabre saluted his poodles as they raced back to the ranks, their job done. The flames now licking against the house were reflected in the cruel gleam of his eyeballs. The blaze gathered pace.

Lisa was still up on the top floor of the house. She took careful aim with a Zulu spear. One of the flaming beach balls exploded with a bang, extinguishing its flames in the process.

Taking this as their cue, Cuthbert and Fatima hurried to the window, armed with bows and arrows. The beach balls made easy targets for the Gruesome Twosome. One by one they were dispatched until all that remained of the poodles' attack was a carpet of deflated rubber and a few puffs of acrid smoke. Round one to the Gruesome Twosome!

CHAPTER FIFTY

Nightmarish Events Continue

WITCHMART MAGAZINE

FOR SALE: Broom. Fully taxed and insured. One evil owner, 22,000 airmiles only. Extras including hagbag, spare bristles, night lights.

Contact Fenella Fengshooey on: crystalball 4360757

On Macabre's command, Badhagg prepared to enter the fray. She was wearing a pair of large, infrared goggles, and was mounting her favourite broom – her Multi-capabilty Fighting Broom!

A downward push of her boot kick-started the twin-cam motor into life. A switch was flicked and two enormous gun-barrels ground slowly into view, aligned along either side of the broom shaft.

Two clowns, acting as ground crew, removed the chocks and the witch taxied out across the garden, ready for take-off.

"Nab those kids!" shouted Macabre.

"Nab those kids!" repeated a group of clowns, strongmen, and flame-singed poodles.

Together they watched as Badhagg's broom climbed steeply into the sky. The Remarkable Otto broke off from trying to bend Mrs Hubbard's wrought-iron gates, in order to admire the spectacle.

Fatima too, was watching from an upstairs window.

"Badhagg!" she shouted to her brother. "Mounted on fighter broom!"

"Then let us not tarry, sis!"

They raced up the stairs, raising clouds of dust as they went.

"Where are you two going?" Lisa called out.

"To take on Badhagg!" came the reply.

Cuthbert and Fatima on the roof. A damp chill in the air, winding around the fog-bound garden. Hearts pitter-pattering with fear. But battle was now joined and fears had to be overcome.

Fatima led her brother across the parapet, to where two cross-eyed, moss-covered gargoyles stood guard over a pair of ancient ornamental cannon. In the distance they could hear the drone of Badhagg's broom, climbing overhead. Time was running out. Cuthbert moved a raindrenched tarpaulin and there lay a pile of seven or eight shining black cannonballs.

"Bingo!"

Badhagg was smiling. It felt wonderful to be out and about on this damp and dismal Halloween night, up to nastiness and no-goodery. These were the nights all bad witches dreamed of! If only she weren't following Macabre's orders, and could be free to do as she pleased. The witch turned to brooding, which ended only when she switched on her in-broom stereo system. *The Witch Queen of Halloween!* pounded out from tiny speakers.

Badhagg made a sudden turn to the left, banking steeply, and then began her descent towards Mrs Hubbard's house. She fired her first round, a quick burst, just to get the range.

FAKATAKATAK!

Tracer lights zipped through the gloom, laser sharp, lightning bright. Seconds later the bullets exploded on to the roof, dislodging a number of roof-tiles located close to where Cuthbert and Fatima had positioned themselves.

Fatima glanced across at Cuthbert, her eyes twitching with determination. "Wait until you see the red of her eyes!"

Spying her quarry down on the roof, Badhagg turned and roared in for another attack. This time the blast from her guns found their target. A large chimney pot exploded beside Cuthbert, and rolled off the roof.

Trying to stay calm and focused, Fatima aimed her cannon at the fast-approaching hag. She made a difficult target, what with the fog and the way the broom was zigzagging back and forth.

Cuthbert covered his ears in alarm. Fatima took aim and fired. The cannonball sailed harmlessly wide of

Badhagg's approaching broom. The witch gave a wicked and largely toothless laugh.

Cuthbert, nervous and hands all-a-shake, looked through the sights of his cannon, waited until he could see the witch's eyes widening in triumph, then fired.

BOOOM!

The broom was hit! A puff of smoke cleared to reveal Badhagg, struggling to maintain control. The course of her broom had become very erratic, veering first to the left and then to the right. Badhagg glanced back and saw to her alarm that her bristles were alight.

"Good shooting," grinned Fatima.

"Our aim proved true," agreed Cuthbert, as they made their way from the roof. "It was ever thus."

Lisa was waiting to add her own congratulations. "Nice work! They'll think twice before trying that again!"

Maybe. But Macabre wasn't done yet.

CHAPTER FIFTY-ONE

A Direct Hit

"There was a loud bang," sobbed Mr Spangly, his make-up wet with tears.

Macabre's followers looked forlornly at the sky for any sign of the witch and her broom.

Directly above them, a flustered, warty-handed Badhagg was hastily strapping on a parachute. Dark, dieselly smoke made her splutter and choke. With a bad-tempered curse, she leapt from the burning broom, which carried on flying for a few seconds, before finally plummeting earthwards. It made an excruciating sound as it fell. Like screaming cats.

Heads turned upwards, clowns were in tears, lions and poodles howling in unison.

Meanwhile, Badhagg's parachute opened to reveal that it was actually an oversized pair of silk pantaloons. She floated almost gracefully down to the ground, muttering to herself as she went. "The time is almost come when I shall suffer these indignities no more!"

Mrs Hubbard looked out and noticed the broom as it fell. "My oh my, the stars are bright tonight!"

Trailing a plume of smoke and flame, the witch's broom plunged straight into the roof of 22a Gravestone Walk, demolishing what remained of the chimney on the way. The roof juddered on impact, but thankfully for those sheltering below, held firm.

Badhagg was now at tree level, and watched her favourite broom, or what was left of it, vanish from view.

"Another ten seconds and I 'ad 'em!" she growled to herself and started to tug at the pantaloonchute in order to steer herself towards a decent landing spot.

CHAPTER FIFTY-TWO

Strangers in the Night

CALLER TO DOGSTOOTH COMMUNITY
RADIO STATION, 1.15 a.m.

"It's about all those calls about Windflower, Deke.
Some folks 'as been sayin' there ain't no power an'
all, well I jest drove through an' it looked fine to me,
ah seen most the folks all up the fairground there'n
they all looking like they're havin' a great time. Only
thing is that fog is layin' there pretty heavy, so you
gotta drive real careful. Say, Deke, could you play a
song for my Geena?"

"Sure, caller."

"I'd like you all to play that there 'Strangers in the
Night', 'cos that's her favourite."

"'Strangers in the Night' it is."

Whilst Macabre was cursing his troops and
bemoaning their lack of prowess, Badhagg
stumbled into view, her face blackened by smoke, and
still carrying her parachute.

Mr Spangly tried to clean the witch's face with
his water-squeezing carnation, but only received a box

on the ears for his trouble.

"Another failure!" snapped Macabre.

The witch made no reply but stared at the ground with a look that would have frozen fire.

"They keep winning," whimpered Mr Spangly, and then instantly regretted it.

Macabre grabbed him by his piano-key lapels. He whispered into the clown's ear.

"We've tried force. Now we're about to try something more subtle."

"Fire?" suggested Mr Spangly. "Sorry. That wasn't a good suggestion, er –"

Luckily for him Macabre wasn't listening. "There is someone in that house we haven't even considered," he brooded.

Clowns and penguins looked baffled.

". . .the old woman's cat."

"Ah!" clowns and penguins murmured as one.

"In my experience," continued the ringmaster, stroking his moustache, pacing like a caged beast, "a cat will often gain access to the premises by means of. . .?"

Blank expressions on white painted faces.

"A cat flap, you nincompoops! Every fortress has its weakness, and this is theirs."

Badhagg grinned. The old witch knew a good scheme when she heard one. "So what's your plan?" she asked, intrigued despite herself.

"The clowns will attack once more," replied Macabre. "But it will only be a diversion. Meanwhile,

187

you will use the cat flap to gain entry to the house."

Badhagg's oath ensured her compliance. "Consider it done."

Lisa couldn't see much from the dining room window, because the shutters were fastened tight. But she could sense something out there – something menacing. Footsteps were crunching on gravel, and they were drawing closer.

A group of stilted clowns swayed suddenly into view. Evil faces. Deadly carnations. The mist swirling about their giant stilts only lent their appearance an even more terrifying aspect.

Lisa had been joined by Cuthbert and Fatima.

"We've got a problem here," she muttered. "Look!"

Fatima's eyes widened with fear. "They're on stilts! They'll be able to reach in through the windows."

Lisa turned and hurried across the room. "Mrs Hubbard!"

"Yes, my dear?"

"Do you have any gardening tools?"

Mrs Hubbard's snowflake eyes narrowed in thought.

"Gardening tools," repeated Lisa, urgently, for time was short.

"It's a little late in the day for that sort of thing, don't you think? But try looking in the cupboard under the stairs, I do believe we kept some old tools in there."

Lisa ran through to the stairway and quickly found

188

a large walk-in cupboard filled with all sorts of strange antique gardening implements.

"Lisa! They're right outside!" called out Fatima, in alarm.

A clown had begun to tap on an upstairs window, his long nails searching for a loose catch or an unfastened bolt.

Lisa emerged next to Cuthbert and Fatima carrying a large and unexpectedly state-of-the-art chainsaw.

She wound down the blinds a little then signalled to Cuthbert to open the window.

A huge pair of stripy clown's trousers loomed before them. Lisa's heart thumped pitterpatterfast.

With a tug of the cord, the chainsaw whirred into life. The clown, whose name was Giorgio, felt a sudden wobble from down below. Lisa's chainsaw blade was now moving smoothly, if noisily, through his stilts and striped trousers, showering wood chip and candy-stripe in all directions.

"Tim-berrrr!" cried out Cuthbert.

As Giorgio's stilts crashed to the ground, the evil clown was left clawing at the window pane with his fingertips. Slowly and excruciatingly, he began to slide downwards, fingernails extended. They made a hideous sound, those nails on glass, like polystyrene foam, like crying tomcats. Giorgio slid from view and then was seen no more.

"Aaaargh!"

Lisa's eyes blazed defiantly behind the chainsaw. Cuthbert and Fatima looked across and, without speaking, nodded their heads in satisfaction. For the first time since their crazy speedingtrain escape, they now believed that victory was possible. Together with Lisa and Mrs Hubbard they could just . . . maybe . . . take on the Great Macabre and win!

Meanwhile, in the warm and consoling glow of Mrs Hubbard's kitchen, a large flea-ridden tabby strode complacently across the tiles. He continued his sedate progress until he reached the cat flap located at the bottom of the kitchen door, and there he paused. Oliver's ears twitched as he listened to voices coming from the other side. The voices of Macabre and the witch, Badhagg.

"Good kitty, nice kitty. Can we use your cat flap, kitty?"

"Miaow," came the reply.

Macabre grabbed Badhagg's arm. "You'll have to put a spell on to the stupid beast or how will we understand what it's saying?"

Badhagg nodded her head and then thought for a while. "This should do the trick." She muttered a few garbled words and raised her arms above her head.

"Testing, testing," she croaked.

"Testing what?" sneered Oliver from the other side of the flap.

Macabre smiled. "Excellent work." He then shouldered the witch to one side and crouched down by the flap. "Hello, puss. If we can use your cat flap, we'll make it worth your while. What do pussies like? Fish? Pink mice? A fur-lined basket?"

"Five thousand in used notes," replied Oliver, cool as you like.

Macabre spluttered with outrage. "Five thousand!" He said it again. "FIVE thousand!"

Badhagg was just as shocked. "Five thousand? Just to use a filthy cat flap?"

Oliver gave a low, resonant purr and examined each of his front paws in turn. He whispered back through the flap again. "Five thousand, or I tip off the others about your little plan."

On the other side of the door, Macabre's face was contorting into a hideous shape. "Very well. Very well then, pussy cat. You drive a hard bargain, but it's a deal. Five thousand it is."

He turned to Badhagg and hissed into her ear. "Remind me to feed that fleabag to the lions once we're inside."

Badhagg nodded in agreement but Macabre was already striding back towards the Carnival Train in search of the money. Since business had fallen off he wasn't sure he had that kind of cash, but he knew where the clowns kept their savings. That would do nicely.

Mrs Hubbard had entered the kitchen and was looking across at Oliver, still crouched by the flap.

"My dear old Ollykins, whatever are you up to? This is no night to go strollabout."

At that very moment, as Oliver looked round and

Mrs Hubbard spoke, a large wad of very dirty fifty pennywig notes dropped through the cat flap.

CHAPTER FIFTY-THREE

Mainly Concerning Cats

In an upper hallway, Cuthbert and Fatima shivered as though some evil deed had just been done, and muttered one word. "Oliver!"

Lisa knew enough about these tiny souls to know that they didn't make things up. They were as finely tuned as the aerial on Sheriff Cohnberg's car. If they felt betrayed then something bad was about to happen.

"The kitchen," muttered Cuthbert with grim forboding. "Something evil enters in."

Lisa grabbed her Zulu spear, a large wicker shield, a swig of strong coffee, and led the way, as they sprinted down dusty corridors and creaking steps, towards the warm and very cosy kitchenglow.

Badhagg was already halfway through the cat flap. Skinny old crone though she was, and even with a spell to ease her passage through the opening, the flap was still a tight squeeze. To try and make things easier, Badhagg poked her globe through the flap first, and then began to force her head and shoulders through the gap. On the other side of the kitchen, Oliver was watching her progress.

Mrs Hubbard found herself completely distracted by the sight of the globe, glowing and bright. To her dim, age-dulled eyes, it looked like some giant Christmas decoration. She crossed the floor and picked it up.

"What a pretty thing!" the old lady enthused on picking up the globe. Its glow completely hypnotized her.

Badhagg's face flushed purple with rage. She hated anyone touching her crystal ball.

"Give that back, you old fool! Don't mess with things you don't understand!"

Mrs Hubbard, still in something of a trance, handed the globe to Fatima, who had just arrived next to her. This only enraged the witch still further.

"Hey! This is not some crummy game of pass-the-parcel! That globe has been in my family for three centuries, now give it back, before I get nasty!" By now, Badhagg had managed to haul the rest of her body through the flap. Her ragged robes still smelled of smoke from the burned broom.

She fixed the Gruesome Twosome with an ugly look. "Hello, Cuthbert. Hello, Fatima. My dear children. How nice to see you both again. How we've all *missed* you."

Lisa noticed how long the witch's nails were and how wrinkled her hands, like toadskin.

Badhagg wanted to cast a spell right there, but of course she couldn't because Fatima had hold of her precious crystal ball.

Badhagg turned and tried to unlock the kitchen door. As it creaked slowly open, Cuthbert and Fatima recognized at once the blood-red jacket and blackasnight top hat of their nemesis, Macabre.

For a moment the twins flapped helplessly, like magician's doves, uncertain as to whether or not to fly.

"My babies!" cried Macabre, gleefully. "It's time to return home."

Cuthbert and Fatima turned tail and ran. Fatima still clutching the witch's globe.

Hearts pounding.

Heads swimming.

Legsrunasfastasyoucan.

Lisa grabbed hold of Mrs Hubbard and they raced after their friends. For the first time she'd seen the Great Macabre in the flesh and the sight chilled her to the bone.

"After them!" shouted the ringmaster, waving his whip angrily. "This time they shall not escape!"

CHAPTER FIFTY-FOUR

WITCHMART MAGAZINE

FOR SALE: one crystal ball. V.g.c except for slight crack. Can see up to one week in future or past. Will also cast spells. Search facility.
Contact Gisella Greenspawn, Coven 233232 or witchmail: spelz@blackcrags.crone.uk

The Gruesome Twosome could move fast when they needed to. Lisa and Mrs Hubbard could hardly keep up. Through the kitchen, back down dusty corridors, left at the broken sofa, into the hallway where the huge chandelier dangled precariously, crowned with dripping, ancient candles.

But Macabre and his followers were hot on their trail. Lisa could hear the hoot of bicycle horns and the screech of Badhagg's crazed laughter.

Macabre emerged at the foot of the stairs, breathless and enraged. He cracked his whip and looked around for the fleeing escapees.

"No use hiiii—ding!" he sang.

He glimpsed Fatima at the top of the stairs. She still had hold of the witch's globe.

"Where did they get that from?" spluttered the ringmaster, his face distorted with anger and impatience.

Badhagg suddenly appeared at his shoulder, clucking like an angry and very ugly hen. "It was all his fault!"

She pointed down at Oliver, who for the first time, seemed to lose his usual air of cocky self-assurance. So much so that he was in the process of making a run for it when one of Macabre's long arms shot out and grabbed him by the tail.

"A treacherous tabby, hmmmm? Well we don't care for that! Take this flea-bag to the Carnival Train and introduce him to the rest of his family tree!"

Mr Spangly looked uncertain. "Family tree?"

"The lions," sneered Macabre. "And let that be a lesson to all who dare to cross Finian Macabre!"

A clown in a green and yellow checked jacket emerged to spirit away the luckless puss.

Out in the night air it was cold. Lisa squeezed through the roof-light leading from the attic and then extended a hand down to Cuthbert and Fatima.

"Well done, guys."

"Guys?" came a querying reply.

Lisa found herself holding an unexpectedly wrinkled old hand. It was Mrs Hubbard.

"Guys and plucky old citizen," Lisa corrected herself.

"That's better, my dear. Now where is Oliver?"

Lisa's heart sank. It wasn't going to be easy to explain to Mrs Hubbard that her beloved cat was a vile traitor. "Er, I haven't seen him for a while – cats – you know what they're like. . ." Lisa trailed off in mid-sentence, but her answer seemed to have satisfied the old lady.

Lisa turned to Fatima, who was still clutching Badhagg's globe.

"Is there any way you could use that crystal ball to get us off this roof and somewhere safe?"

Fatima's expression didn't offer much in the way of hope. "Of her spells we know very few."

Lisa ran her fingers through her hair, and tried not to panic. "You don't know *any* spells then?"

"We can summon rain," Cuthbert enthused. "But only in Spain."

Lisa pointed at the crystal ball, which right now looked as innocent and unmagical as a goldfish bowl.

"So no chance of using this thing to fly us off the roof?"

"Perhaps," mumbled Fatima nervously, "perhaps an outside chance."

Lisa placed a hand on her bony shoulder. "Just give it your best shot."

CHAPTER FIFTY-FIVE

TRANSCRIPT, DOGSTOOTH COMMUNITY
RADIO STATION, 3.10 a.m.

"Through the night here with me, Howlin' Deke
Wilkins. That was the sound of Tammy Burnett
and her 'Cheatin' Green Eyes'. Still grey and misty
out there, so y'all mind how you go. Freeway
sixty-six, a few problems there . . . we got a report
of a wild poodle on the loose . . . I think I'm
reading that right. . . I guess that's just the boys in
the newsroom here havin' a little fun. That right
boys? Heeheehee. . ."

Inside Mrs Hubbard's home, so recently invaded by
the Circus Army, Macabre was deep in conversation
with two tall, very muscular men, whose twirly
moustaches were even longer than his own. These
were the Brothers Fantoni, experts in gymnastical
pyrotechnics.

Four penguins struggled into view, carrying a large
powerfully sprung trampoline. The Fantoni Brothers
(whose first names no one knew), began to fasten on

their matching helmets, and then rubbed chalk on to the palms of their giant hands.

Fatima and Cuthbert were muttering more and more spells, but nothing seemed to be working.

"Couldn't we just climb down?" asked Mrs Hubbard.

Lisa inched cautiously to the edge of the roof and peered down. It was a sheer drop. And at the bottom of it all, still wreathed in dense fog, were Macabre's Army: clowns, ferocious poodles, strongman and fire-eater, penguins and hungry, flea-bitten lions.

Back inside the old house, the Brothers Fantoni had finished limbering up. Now they mounted the trampoline, bouncing and backflipping extravagantly. Their broad moustaches appeared to give them added lift and stability, acting, perhaps, as primitive rudders.

Higher and higher they bounced, now almost on a level with what had once been Mrs Hubbard's chandelier, now to within a milli-inch of the beautifully decorated plasterwork on her ceiling. Then, the mightiest bounce of all: a great crescendo on the monkey's drums was followed by the sight of the brothers crashing straight through the ceiling.

SMASH! Up through the timber floor of the loft. . .

SMASH! All the way to the roof itself! (It was fortunate for them that they were wearing helmets. . .)

One of the Fantonis, though slightly stunned by the succession of impacts, landed right by Lisa's side. He looked at her with rotating pupils and then, before she could move, grabbed her round the waist and vanished back through the newly-made hole in the roof.

"Lisa!" screamed Cuthbert and Fatima.

But she had already disappeared from the trampoline below and into the arms of the Remarkable Otto, Circus Strongman. He held her like he wasn't about to let go.

"Lisa!" cried Fatima, gazing wide-eyed and frightened through the hole in the roof.

Cuthbert looked equally lost. "Miss Palermo! Come back!"

Fatima seized her brother by the arm and led him from the gaping hole in the ceiling. "Be careful . . . they might come back for *us*."

"What will they do to Lisa?" asked Cuthbert, and his face looked even more full of woes than usual.

Fatima didn't answer but her pained expression told him all he needed to know.

How the Great Macabre delighted in the sight of the frightened Lisa captured and on parade; Lisa frightened and not knowing what was coming next! He removed his hat, and then bowed with an absurdly long flourish in front of her.

"Glad to finally meet you, my dear," he hissed through his newly-waxed moustache.

"You'll never get away with this!" protested Lisa, very scared. If only half the things she'd heard about Macabre were true then she was in big trouble.

Macabre laughed at her obvious terror.

"You have very nice teeth," he leered. "Did anyone ever tell you that?"

Lisa shook her head, a little confused.

The ringmaster's hat had begun to grow larger and larger. So large that when Macabre held it over Lisa, it covered her whole body. The hat then began to shrink again. Macabre put it back on his head. Lisa had vanished inside the hat like a magician's rabbit!

There was a round of applause from the watching Circus Army, (except for Badhagg, who gave a sniff and looked in the other direction). Macabre answered the applause with an immodest bow.

"What now, chief?" asked Mr Spangly.

"Now we return to the fairground with the lovely Lisa in tow, and wait for those tiresome twins to follow."

"Will they do that?"

"Of course," replied the ringmaster. "Because they've got big hearts. Fools like them always have big hearts. That's why they never win. Hahahahahahahah!!!"

CHAPTER FIFTY-SIX

The Team Divides

On the roof of her crumbling, under-siege home, Mrs Hubbard was angrily strapping on a metal helmet. Lisa's sudden capture seemed to have roused her to action.

"Well don't just stand there, children! Are we going to let them get away with that? Let's get after those hoodlums!"

There was a long pause before Fatima spoke again, her voice much weaker than before. "Macabre wants us to follow him. That's his plan, I know it."

"But Lisa is your teacher, children," pleaded Mrs Hubbard (still not understanding), tears a-glisten in her eyes. "And your friend."

Cuthbert shuffled his feet nervously from side to side. They'd never had a friend before, and now they did they certainly didn't want to lose her.

"Better to die in valour than live in shame," he suddenly announced.

Now it was Fatima who appeared the more hesitant. "Perhaps if we followed . . . at a safe distance . . . just to see where they have taken her?"

Cuthbert nodded.

Mrs Hubbard was on the point of joining them in their mission when her fadedsnowflakeeyes suddenly clouded.

"But what about my Oliver? What if he were to return and find no one at home?"

Her eyes softened to the point of tears. "Who would give him his tea? It's mackerel today . . . and who would wipe his little whiskers clean?"

Fatima took Mrs Hubbard's old thin hand into her own cold thin hand and gave it a rub. "You stay here, Mrs Hubbard. Don't worry about us. We'll bring Lisa back."

Cuthbert issued a word of warning to the old lady. "But do not open your doors to anyone of strange report."

Mrs Hubbard nodded. "I'm on my guard, my dears, now I know what wickedness we are up against."

Fatima's thoughts were suddenly interrupted by a frightening sound: CLANG! CLANG!

The Carnival Train was about to depart again. Loud whistles announced the moment. And Cuthbert and Fatima guessed at once who would be on board . . . Lisa! A prisoner of the Great Macabre and, likely as not, frightened out of her wits. She wasn't as used as they were to the circus. Things would seem even more terrifying to a newcomer, they feared.

Cuthbert, Fatima, and Mrs Hubbard had descended to the front door of the house and were looking out on the mist-strewn garden, stretching to the graveyard in the distance. They saw Macabre's train slide off into the gloom, the Circus Army all aboard.

Without further ado the Gruesome Twosome mounted their pogo-sticks, which they had cleverly kept hidden beneath a holly bush by the front porch.

"Tally Ho!" cried Cuthbert. "Eyes on the road, dearest sis, the mist lies thick tonight and at no cost must we lose the trail."

"Don't worry, I can see sparks and steam up ahead."

"And the sound of iron and steel. Farewell, Mrs Hubbard!"

"Farewell, my dears," came the reply, already distant. "And good luck!"

CHAPTER FIFTY-SEVEN

More Train-spotting

The giant smokeandsparkle Carnival Train clickety-clacked its way to the Fairgound by the sea, travelling not on tracks, as most trains did, but over silver-dewed earth and hoar-frosted fields.

Inside Macabre's private compartment, garishly lit by swaying orange lanterns, stood Lisa. She was guarded on both sides by two burly clowns. Her eyes scanned the room, slowly taking in the surroundings. There were posters on the wall: faded, frightening images of performers past and present. In another corner lay a pile of half deflated black balloons. Lisa then heard the sound of approaching footsteps. The door swung open and in swaggered the Great Macabre. He stared at Lisa with winepink eyes. Thousands of tiny cracks in his make-up. An odour of cheap aftershave.

"Soon you'll be one of us," he hissed. "It will be most pleasing to see a beauty such as yourself performing beneath the Big Top. Assisting perhaps, your new friends, the Gruesome Twosome. They throw knives you know. One or two might well fly in your direction. And since they haven't practised in a while, who is to say whether or not they might not miss occasionally. Oh, dear! Poor Lisa! Haha-haha!"

His laugh was loud and cruel, like the mechanical laughter outside a fairground stall. It echoed out into the night, above the sounds of the Carnival Train with its cages full of wild beasts, sobbing clowns, and mad penguins.

Though Cuthbert and Fatima were still on Lisa's trail, so much bouncing on pogo-sticks was beginning to take its toll.

"Any sign of the train?" called out Fatima. "I can't see any more, my eyeballs are jumping!"

"Mine too."

Fatima switched on the fog light mounted on the front of her stick.

"This mist is not from nature come," observed Cuthbert.

"Another Badhagg spell, I bet."

But then, when all seemed lost, Cuthbert spotted the lights of a Big Wheel turning slowly up ahead.

"The fairground!"

The twins stopped and dismounted.

"Remember what Lisa saw there. Danger lies amidst the candyfloss," whispered Cuthbert.

"We will proceed with caution," agreed his sister. "First we must be certain that the Carnival Train has indeed returned here."

They listened for clues, but all they could hear was

the fairground, and then, beyond that, the roar of a distant sea.

Sheriff Cohnberg was seated next to Mr Chesney Dempster, owner of the local newspaper. Moving together as if choreographed, they both bit into their giant hot-dogs and simultaneously slurped on soft drinks. Looked up at the Ferris Wheel, turning slowly in the misty skies above. Still sleepwalking under the witch's spell, they then headed towards the Wall of Death.

Not even sticking a giant hat-pin in him would have roused the lawman or his friends from their trance.

This was the eerie world into which Cuthbert and Fatima had newly entered, first slipping effortlessly between the railings of the perimeter fence, now crouched beneath the generator van, hearts pounding, lips dry, staringeyes.

"I can't hear the train any more. It must have stopped somewhere nearby," whispered Fatima.

"I'm frightened," answered Cuthbert. "'Twas our plan, I thought, to escape the circus, not return to it?"

Fatima thought hard before replying. She too felt very afraid. More than she could remember in a long time, because she knew how terrible Macabre's revenge would be if they were caught now. But at the same time she didn't want to say anything that would encourage Cuthbert into thinking they could just run away. Something inside Fatima told her that the time for flight was over. They would have to find a way of defeating Macabre or they would be hiding from him for ever. But while she was thinking all this, her legs, too, had turned to stone. She wanted to stay here, secure in their running place by the comforting hum of the generator and the darkness of shadows.

Cuthbert was curled almost into a ball, his head tucked into his chest, as though he were just about to be fired from a cannon.

"We are by the sea, could we not find a boat and sail away to a bright and promising future?"

Fatima knew nothing about boats. She had never even seen one, except in the books that she used to read in the Bearded Lady's compartment when there was no one else around. She remembered a beautiful ocean liner with three bright red funnels and a hundred piece orchestra. Its name was the *Titanic* and she had always dreamed of making a voyage on such a ship, with endless nights of luxury in a beautiful cabin, with fine food and hot baths and running water.

"Can we go now?" asked Cuthbert, his voice down in his boots.

Fatima thought of a great liner sailing across the sea to freedom, and then of Lisa, held somewhere in Macabre's evil grasp. "Lisa saved us, you know that?"

Cuthbert made no reply.

"No one ever showed us kindness until we met Lisa and Mrs Hubbard. And they risked their lives to give us shelter."

"No. They fought from fear of Macabre, just as we."

What if Cuthbert were right? Again Fatima thought of escape. Of running away, sailing across the sea, until they reached somewhere not even the Carnival Train could follow. Happy thoughts. But impossible ones. She knew Macabre and she knew he would never, ever give up. He'd stick to them like wallpaper paste. He'd always be right behind them, like the tear in the seat of a clown's pants.

"No, Cuthbert. No more running away."

Cuthbert looked up and for one awful, falling-from-the-trapeze moment, Fatima thought he was about to leave her.

"Tell me then, how we can rescue fair Lisa and yet extricate ourselves from our present peril?"

Fatima reached into her bag. "Remember, we still have this."

Cuthbert's eyes brightened. "Badhagg's crystal ball!"

Fatima nodded. "Exactly. All is not lost yet!"

Cuthbert and Fatima suddenly had to crouch down as a giant clown on stilts walked by, armed with a gun; his shadow cast them, for a moment, into total darkness.

Inside the Carnival Train, Lisa found herself listening to the sounds of the fairground rides. . .

Hurdygurdysandwaltzers, everything outoftune and nothingquiteright.

She was still being held captive inside the Carnival

Train, locked inside a small compartment where the only source of light was a single, spluttering lantern fashioned in the shape of a clown's head.

To guard her, Macabre had detailed two ferocious penguins armed with sink-plunger guns.

She was struggling to stay awake, unaware that Macabre had ordered Badhagg to send her to sleep. She fought the spell as best she could, eyes growing heavy, but it was so long since she'd slept. "I must stay awake, I must. . ."

The mist descended over Lisa and she fell into a deep slumber, black hair curled over closed eyes, hardly breathing. Moments later, two clowns entered the compartment and carried her off.

CHAPTER FIFTY-EIGHT

A Near Miss

Barrabas's search for the circus was almost at an end. Moving first through the deserted streets of Windflower, the trail led next to the old fairground. It was easy enough to find, for its lights were the only ones for miles around, and the whole population seemed to be assembling there.

"This is a strange place," Barrabas grumbled to Blackdog. "No one speaks." He had just shown the picture of Cuthbert and Fatima to a young girl with her hair in a ponytail and dull, lifeless eyes.

"Have you, by any chance, ever come across two tiny tots who look like this? Except by now they will be ten years older. . . ."

The girl made no reply but bit on her toffee apple. . . Toffee apple!

Only now did Barrabas realize he was already outside the funfair, for everywhere there was candyfloss, and toffee apples and ice-cold drinks. But what about clowns and circus folk? Were there any of them there too?

Blackdog led the way as they entered through a large gateway, guarded by a two-headed fire-eater, the flames of whose breath lit up a sign:

THIS FAIRGROUND WAS OPENED ON
12TH JUNE, 19--
BY
MRS HIRAM DODGEM

IT HAS BEEN CREATED PRIMARILY FOR THE ENJOYMENT OF THE
CITIZENS AND CHILDREN OF WINDFLOWER, BUT VISITORS TO OUR
TOWN ARE MOST WELCOME TO SHARE ITS PLEASURES.

THE COMMITTEE

Barrabas and Blackdog were moving amidst a sea of faces, all winding their way around the fairground.

Blank eyes, no expression.

EveryonewiththeHalloweenblues.

A young boy in a skeleton costume had given him a coconut, and the lighthouse keeper clutched it under his coat as he tried to find news of his missing offspring.

"Have you, by any chance, ever come across two tiny tots who look like this? Except by now they will be ten years older. . ."

There was no response.

"Nobody knows anything, Blackdog," sighed Barrabas.

Blackdog nuzzled closer, as if trying to console his new master.

Barrabas found himself standing at the entrance to the Ghost Train ride. In front of him, a spooky painting showed a train being driven by a deathly-looking skeleton clad in a black hood and carrying a sickle. Barrabas thought the ride looked far too frightening for little children, though there seemed plenty who disagreed. Two kids were already sitting in one of the Ghost Train's open-topped carriages, ready for the ride to begin. They looked the same sort of age that Cuthbert and Fatima would now be.

Barrabas hurried forward, eager to speak with them, just as the train was about to move. An evil-eyed penguin handed him a ticket and seemed to look the lighthouse keeper suspiciously up and down. Barrabas climbed into a carriage directly behind the two youngsters, heart full of hope, and gripped the iron bars as the ghost train twitched into life. Blackdog hesitated then leapt into the seat alongside his master.

Two doors burst open ahead, painted with hellish flames, revealing a black void, and the train lurched forward towards it. Barrabas almost lost his cap. . .

No sooner had the Ghost Train vanished off on its juddering, careering, heart-in-mouth journey, than two pale and frightened figures emerged next to the entrance, exactly where Barrabas and Blackdog had been standing.

Cuthbert and Fatima were still looking for Lisa and the Circus Army but it was proving difficult to search the fairground whilst keeping themselves out of sight too. It meant creeping from ride to ride, hanging in the shadows, trying to blend in. It was guerrilla warfare.

Eyesinthebackofyourheadtime.

"We still have the crystal ball," whispered Fatima. "That may tell us where they have taken Lisa."

Cuthbert made to produce the globe but Fatima stopped him in his tracks.

"Not here. . ."

The penguin at the Ghost Train ticket counter was giving them the evil eye. But by using their small size and nimble feet, the Gruesome Twosome melted back into the crowd and the shadows before the suspicious bird could waddle into action. Nevertheless an alarm of sorts was raised, and extra clowns combed the area.

So it was that whilst the lighthouse keeper Barrabas O'Hanlon plunged through the darkness of the Ghost Train . . . coffinlids, Egyptiandead, dancing spiders, mummies, cobwebs and thrills . . . the Gruesome Twosome were hiding in the shadows of the Big Wheel itself. Alternate spokes of light and darkness. Barrabas was hoping that the two kids seated in front of him might be his own flesh and blood. Cuthbert and Fatima gazing into the witch's globe searching for any sign of Lisa; neither party knowing that they were within touching distance of one another, a father and child reunion so near and yet so far. . .

CHAPTER FIFTY-NINE

```
┌─────────────────────────────────────────┐
│                                           │
│               WARNING                     │
│                                           │
│  * Please observe all safety procedures,  │
│  and note that horseplay and japes will   │
│  not be tolerated. They can affect the    │
│  safety of your fellow passengers.        │
│                                           │
│  * No food to be consumed on rides of a   │
│  topsy-turvy nature.                      │
│                                           │
│  * Please enjoy the rides and be          │
│  considerate to other users.              │
│                                           │
│  * Customers travelling on these rides    │
│  do so at their own risk.                 │
│                                           │
│  * In the event of death or excessive     │
│  excitement, the council will not be held │
│  responsible.                             │
│                                           │
│  WINDFLOWER FAIRGROUND COMMITTEE,         │
│  JAN 12, 19– –.                           │
│                                           │
└─────────────────────────────────────────┘
```

WARNING

* Please observe all safety procedures, and note that horseplay and japes will not be tolerated. They can affect the safety of your fellow passengers.

* No food to be consumed on rides of a topsy -turvy nature.

* Please enjoy the rides and be considerate to other users.

* Customers travelling on these rides do so at their own risk.

* In the event of death or excessive excitement, the council will not be held responsible.

WINDFLOWER FAIRGROUND COMMITTEE, JAN 12, 19– –.

*L*isa woke from the witch's spell, feeling chilled by the night air. The comparative comfort of the train compartment had been replaced by an icy mist and the sense of something hard and cold beneath her spine – rails!

"Tighten those ropes!" snarled Macabre, razorteeth sharp and gleaming against the fairgroundlights, manic eyes bulging. Mr Spangly and the Remarkable Otto started to carry out his instructions, but Lisa suddenly realized her peril and began struggling. She had no intention of being tied to the tracks of the roller-coaster ride without a fight.

"Get off me!" She kicked and punched. "Leave me alone!" At one point she almost broke free. But Otto and Mr Spangly, together, were too strong for her.

Macabre advanced a little closer. Partly to inspect the knots binding her, and partly to gloat. The shadow of his huge top hat fell across Lisa's face.

"Don't think you're the star of the show, my dear, I'm afraid you're only the bait. Just a human honeypot to draw your friends into my trap."

An awful smile crossed Macabre's cracked and unlovely lips. He made a cutting motion across his throat. "But if they don't show up, of course, you might end up looking rather gruesome yourself!"

"The Carnival Train will run over you," interjected Mr Spangly, with a cheerful hoot of his horn.

Macabre pushed his sidekick away and sidled closer to hiss his goodbyes. "Farewell, my lovely. You're a credit to the local police force."

"I'm not in the police," snapped Lisa, defiantly. "And you won't get away with this!"

Lisa could see Macabre's breath, rising in clouds, into the night air, just like the smoke from his own hateful steam train, which even now was preparing to set off along the rickety wooden tracks of the ride.

"In the sad but likely event that we do not meet again, may I also say that you have the most lovely white teeth. Did anyone ever tell you that?"

"Get lost!" snapped Lisa. She wondered if she'd gone too far, but the ringmaster hardly seemed to notice. Within seconds he and Mr Spangly had followed the Remarkable Otto on to a small track maintenance vehicle, and were heading squeakily off to join the rest of the army waiting on the Carnival Train.

Lisa considered her position. *The perfect end to the perfect Halloween*, she thought, with irony, still struggling with the circus ropes binding her to the rails. She had been left at the highest point of the figure of eight circuit, which might have afforded a superb view of the whole fairground, were it not for the fact that she was lying on her back, unable to look at anything except sky. Dark, menacing, Halloween sky.

The Ghost Train containing Barrabas and Blackdog had just crashed through another set of garishly painted doors and was suddenly back in the open air. He was seated in the third carriage from the end. As

218

the train swung out on to the booth he clambered out, apparently unshaken by the experience. His new companion, Blackdog, seemed to possess the same sanguine nature as his master. He hadn't barked once during the ghost ride. The only thing that bothered the lighthouse keeper's dog were the circus folk. Every time one of their number came into view, his hackles would rise and he'd utter a low growl.

Barrabas for his part had seen far more frightening things in his life than a make-believe ghost train ride, however terrifying, but what did upset him was the realization that the two kids seated in front of him were not his own beloved sprogs. One was a ginger-haired girl called Shelley Buchanan, the other a pale-faced youngster with no front teeth. Their dead-eyed gaze looked past him into the distance as he enquired after the twins. Not only did they know nothing of Cuthbert and Fatima, they seemed to know nothing of the Circus Macabre either. Disappointed but ever determined, the lighthouse keeper strode off towards the hall of mirrors to continue his search.

Cuthbert and Fatima were staring at Badhagg's ball, which had once more reverted to its passive, frosty state.

"I'm sure I saw Lisa there a moment ago, but now there's nothing." She gave the ball a determined polish.

"Perhaps Lisa is not here," whispered Cuthbert.

"Perhaps she escaped. She is very clever."

Fatima would love to have believed that. If Lisa really was free, then there would be no need to confront Macabre at all.

Suddenly the globe began to glow again. Fatima grabbed the orb back and watched as a picture began to form within. In fact it was much more than just a picture. It was their world. As real as anything around them.

"The roller-coaster!" gasped Fatima.

"Lisa!" gasped Cuthbert.

The crystal ball had indeed revealed to them the terrifying sight of Lisa Palermo, tied to the roller-coaster's track, hundreds of feet in the air. Petrified. Alone. In peril on the rails.

Cuthbert's heart sank, for he knew at once what they must do, and though he knew it was right, still fear stole into his boots and made them like lead.

Fatima took hold of her brother's hand and led the way, the great silhouette of the roller coaster towering above them as they advanced.

"Courage, brother."

"'It will come to me. It always does in the end."

And in truth, it usually did. Cuthbert had performed as a Bouncing Babe, bouncing so high on the trampoline that young mothers couldn't look; as a toddler he had been fired from the mouths of cannons; as an infant put his tousled head into the mouths of lions; and then finally, as part of the Gruesome Twosome, he had been part of the knife-throwing act.

Blindfold, frightened, throwing knives until they ringed his sister like a second skin.

Cuthbert and Fatima kept to the shadows as they hurried along. They darted past coconut shies and dodgem rides, flitted past fortune-tellers and candy-floss stalls. Everywhere there were guards and spies. At one point Olga the Bearded Lady strode past and Cuthbert was forced to hide his face behind a giant toffee apple. Two sharptoothed poodles snarled on patrol.

The roller-coaster now lay up ahead. There was a small, deserted ticket office, around which the zombified inhabitants of Windflower were wandering aimlessly back and forth. What the twins were not prepared for was the fearful sight of Macabre's train, sitting on the rails of the ride, and surrounded by thick clouds of steam. All ready to depart!

CHAPTER SIXTY

The lions roared and the clowns were pale
As the evil train rattled down the rails
so children watch out, and parents beware
or Macabre will pluck you from out of thin air.

Traditional children's playground song, Windflower.

"**P**oor Lisa!" mumbled Cuthbert, imagining for a split second the awful result of the Carnival Train colliding with his friend. Tears began to fill his sad, darkhollow eyes. "Is there nothing we can do?"

Fatima looked up at the skeletal form of the roller-coaster ride looming above them like a sinister ship: damp iron, mossy timbers. The whole structure creaking and groaning in the night breeze.

"Too tall to climb," Fatima concluded. "Even the Fantoni Brothers couldn't scale those heights."

"But we have to!" interjected Cuthbert, suddenly. "There is no other way to save our friend."

Fatima looked up again. Up to dizzying heights, half lost in the mist. Taller than the Big Top by far. "Are you sure, bro? You know you don't like heights."

"Then best not to dwell too long in the contemplation," replied Cuthbert, reaching up for the length of damp timber that would begin their climb. "Our friend is in dire peril."

Dire indeed.

The Carnival Train was still hissing, getting up steam, blackbillowing smoke.

CLICKETY-CLACK CLICKETY-CLACK, her pistons began to turn. But the roller-coaster ride was so steep that the locomotive only travelled a few metres before she ground once more to a halt. Not enough steam up.

Olga the Bearded Lady shovelled more fuel into the fire-tender box, fearful of a visit from Macabre. The bear who was driving pulled a metal lever to release the brake. Still the great locomotive didn't move.

Three carriages down, the crimson-coated ringmaster had his head out of the window, screaming into the gathering gloom. "Get stoking, you fatheads! Get stoking!"

Lisa could hear his voice bellowing in the distance, and knew her fate would not be long in coming.

The roller coaster: thrillaminute, up and down, corkscrew, mouth-in-heart, hold on to your hats. The most frightening ride in the Windflower Fairground, its old wooden frame and brightly painted coasters had thrilled visitors since 18—.

But all those thrills and spills, all that excited fear, was as naught compared to the terror felt by Cuthbert and Fatima as they gradually began to scale the wooden frame of the ride. Small, fumbling hands reaching up, searching for something to cling on to. Nervous knees, trembling feet pressed against vertical posts and cross-members.

"Don't look down!" shouted Fatima to her brother, as he forged on ahead.

Cuthbert didn't hear, or if he did, wasn't listening. Fear was driving him on now. He sensed that if he stopped climbing even for a second, he might not be able to go on again. Ever.

Shaking legs, moving determinedly upwards. Move then pause. Just like the day when Macabre forced them to walk the tightrope. Only now they were going even higher.

Dizzying the view for anyone brave enough to look; the stalls and rides glittering in and out of the mist, a maze of dodgem car poles poking up, the distant, silent, ghostly town, a glint of moonlight on restless waves. And unbeknownst to the Gruesome Twosome, their father was down there too, trying to communicate with a cluster of candyfloss-eating locals.

Up ahead lay a great lattice-work of creaking, groaning, mouldering timbers. It was like the skin of a huge whale, alive to the touch, trembling and resonating with every windgust. But there was no time for the twins to dwell on any of this, for on the track above, their friend in peril was about to be crushed beneath the wheels of that blackasnight express with its evil, grinning face.

Meanwhile, in the fairground far below, an alert penguin had spotted the Gruesome Twosome and aimed his sink plunger gun in their direction. The projectile almost parted Cuthbert's hair, and landed with a thump against one of the timber supports. Cuthbert momentarily lost his grip and slid painfully down the moss-covered wood, his fingers frantically fighting for something to hold on to. He landed on Fatima's shoulders and for a moment they hung there together, like two flies trapped in a giant web.

The penguin sniper took aim and fired again.

CHAPTER SIXTY-ONE

Steam Up, Sparks Fly

"You're not really going to run over the police lady, are you?" asked a bowler-hatted clown, close to tears. "You said she was going to work in the ticket office."

"I decided she'd be more use to us where she is," snapped Macabre, still looking out of the window. "Or d'you think she's getting too *tied* to her work?"

Macabre began to laugh, tonsils opening and closing like the tunnel doors of the Ghost Train ride. "She's the bait to spring our trap. Once the Gruesome Twosome show up it doesn't matter what happens to her. I don't care. Maybe she would make a nice meal for Madame Mimi's poodles! Hahahaha!"

His laughter echoed down the line and struck a note of terror into the hearts of all who heard it.

Further down the train, Badhagg the witch was also looking out of the window. What she saw there caused her eyes to pop and her eyebrows to perform somersaults. . .

"The Gruesome Twosome!" She hurried along to tell Macabre the news, but found him in a foul mood.

"Why are we still standing still?" he growled.

"Not enough coal in the boiler," mumbled Mr Spangly into his giant shoes.

Macabre's face began to undergo a transition from white, through pink, arriving via red at a vexed, outraged shade of purple. When finally he spoke, it was like one of the explosions devised by Windflower's founder, the great explosives expert, J T Doodlebug.

"WHAAAAAT? You'd better get this sorted out or I'll tie the lot of you to the engine and you can pull it yourselves!"

Badhagg tried to intervene and tell the ringmaster what she'd seen. "I think you should know, I've just seen—"

"Silence, you old toad!" interrupted Macabre. "Can't you see I have other preoccupations? This is not the time for your dimwitted ramblings!"

Badhagg's eyes flashed an angry, sulphurous yellow as Macabre continued to lambast her, with no thought for either the old crone's feelings or her sensitive hearing.

"You couldn't spell your way out of a paper bag!" he trumpeted.

At this the witch stormed out of the carriage, her own frozen-pond complexion flushing to an angry red. She was in a rage. No one spoke to a witch like that – not even Macabre. She'd come to help and this was how he'd treated her. Well no more! Tonight was Halloween. And the midnight hour was drawing closer. Just minutes away now, she sensed. Scuttling back into her own compartment, she began rummaging through her old files. Seething anger fed her quest. Faded newspapers, cuttings, photographs and etchings, all were cast aside as Badhagg's bony fingers searched back through the years.

"No . . . no . . . no, not that one, no . . . no . . . no . . . mmm. . ."

Suddenly her ugly goggle-eyes widened. Was this what she'd been looking for? It was a parchment. Signed by herself and witnessed by the Great Macabre himself.

"Eureka!"

CHAPTER SIXTY-TWO

*L*uckily for Lisa the Carnival Train was still refusing to move. The bear on the footplate and a team of penguins and clowns were feeding her boilers with coal, but once the fire of such a large locomotive has gone out it can't quickly be rekindled.

And now there was another distraction for the Circus Army – Macabre's sniper penguins had alerted him to the sight of the Gruesome Twosome, climbing towards him. Cuthbert's hand had just reached the first letter "L" in the giant ROLLER-COASTER sign on the side of the ride. Fatima was not far behind. The news of their approach filled Macabre with improved humour.

"You see, my plan has worked! My plan has worked! I've tempted them out into the open and now it's open season. . . A gold-plated unicycle to the first clown to bring down the Gruesome Twosome!"

Of course Macabre didn't have a gold-plated unicycle and, even if he did, he certainly wouldn't have given it away. But the clowns, empty-headed after so many blows to the head with buckets and planks of wood, weren't to know this, and rushed eagerly to the train windows, ready to take aim at Cuthbert and Fatima.

A variety of projectiles began to rain upon the Gruesome Twosome, and Fatima had to take avoiding action. She sheltered for a moment underneath the ride's giant lettering. A gust of wind whistled by, causing the whole structure to rock alarmingly. Fatima's heart beat so fast she thought it might burst.

Looking up she saw that they would soon be alongside the steepest curve of the track, and that the angle of the ride's construction might make them safe from attack, at least for a while.

"We have to stop that train!" shouted Fatima to her sibling as they began to climb again.

"How?"

"I don't know, we'll find a way—" Fatima ducked as another projectile sailed by. A flaming beach ball fired by two poodles. She could feel the flames lick as they passed.

The train began to move. Not very far at first. The initial movement was soon followed by a sharp jolt that threw everyone on board off their feet.

For a second time the Carnival Train had ground to a halt.

For the first time in all these endless years of searching, Barrabas felt he was close to his missing infants. It was in the air. Call it instinct, call it what you like. He had found Macabre's Circus, of that he was now sure. And a fairground full of kids, all the right age.

He saw a clown up ahead. Surely he would know of Macabre's Circus. He might even be part of it. Barrabas ignored Blackdog's uneasy whine and tapped on the clown's shoulder, "Excuse me, sir. . ."

The clown in question, wearing a silver bowler hat, turned on his heels and looked at Barrabas with cold, unblinking eyes. "Not now . . . we're busy watching the train."

"Train?" Barrabas looked up just in time to see a locomotive beginning to move up the track, bell clanging, full steam ahead. . .

The clown had already run off, joined in turn by the other clowns and circus folk. Barrabas ran alongside them.

"Excuse me, sir. . ."

"Go away!"

Mr Dickins, the printer, had been right: these clowns were an ill-mannered crew. The lighthouse keeper found himself almost flattened in some kind of circus stampede. All sorts of strange creatures swept past him: poodles, stilt-walkers, the two-headed fire-eater. All hurrying towards the roller-coaster ride.

Barrabas took out his telescope, more closely to follow the action. He could see the train, not like the sort you normally saw on such an attraction, but a great black beast of a machine, with a painted face, and puffs of black steam billowing forth.

Then, as he zoomed close on the action, Barrabas suddenly gasped a sharp intake of breath. There was someone up there, further down the line, tied to the

231

track: a young woman with black hair and a blue tunic!

Barrabas knew at once what he must do. He was a lighthouse keeper, trained to rescue those in peril.

It was in his blood, like the sea. . .

He turned and was about to begin running towards the disaster scene when something suddenly loomed out of the fog ahead of him. Blackdog barked loudly and sprang forward – too late! Blue sparks and brightshinychrome.

The honk of a horn and then darkness. Barrabas had been knocked down by a dodgem car, and for a long time he lay motionless on the misty and frosted ground while his canine companion whined piteously and tried in vain to wake his master. . .

CHAPTER SIXTY-THREE

To the Rescue

Step by step, with frozen fingers and fearful hearts, the Gruesome Twosome had somehow managed to ascend the giant roller-coaster, scrambling like ants up its huge, rickety frame. Now they could sense the locomotive up ahead. But they couldn't see it. Great plumes of jet-black steam engulfed the whole scene. It was the perfect cover for their assault.

Cuthbert could hear Macabre's voice, raging through the gloom. "Where are the twins? Are they still climbing? Bring lanterns, you fools!"

Fatima was alongside her brother now, while in front of them loomed the Carnival Train, steel wheels, pistons pounding into life, closer and closer it came. . .

"Quickly!" whispered Fatima. "While they can't see us."

Her brother scrambled on to her shoulders and then grabbed at the side of the locomotive. She heard a shrill whistle blast and muffled shouts.

Cuthbert extended a frail arm to his sister and with an agile leap, she joined him on the roof of the Carnival Train. The wind whistled in their hair and thick black smoke filled their lungs.

Without waiting for his sister, Cuthbert ran off down the carriage roof, leaping with great agility as it rocked from side to side. "This way!"

She could hear his voice, but he was already lost in the steam and smoke billowing forth from ancient boilers.

But the Circus Army was alert to the arrival of the Gruesome Twosome, and almost at once, the Remarkable Otto began to climb out of a window in pursuit.

"Halt!" he shouted in his heavy Bavarian accent. "Schtopp vare you are!"

The Remarkable Otto's muscles bulged and his eyebrows were knitted with rage. Fatima avoided a couple of swipes from tattooed and hardaspiston fists.

Somehow, in the struggle, the Remarkable Otto became trapped, his huge frame too large for the opening through which he was trying to squeeze. Fatima managed to dodge past his flailing arms and followed her brother down the roof of the carriage.

"Halt!" screamed Otto. "Vill you defy me?"

Fatima didn't stop to reply. She didn't even turn around. It seemed to her that the train had picked up speed and she knew that time was very short indeed.

CHAPTER SIXTY-FOUR

A Carriage With No View

Macabre stared at the Remarkable Otto's bottom with mounting frustration.

"What are you doing? I told you to get out there and grab them!"

"Ich . . . I . . . am trept, Herr Macabre. . ."

The ringmaster took off his hat and threw it to the floor in a rage.

"Mother was right!" he growled. "It would have been easier to train a circus of fleas!"

"Don't give up!" Lisa had told her kids that often enough. But right now she felt like giving up herself. The ropes around her wouldn't budge and the approaching train was sending vibrations up the line as it drew closer.

The only ray of hope she could find was the thought that somehow, somewhere, Cuthbert and Fatima might be on their way to help her. But she wasn't holding her breath. They were small, frightened kids who'd spent their whole lives trying to escape from Macabre's evil show. Why would they risk their new-won freedom on someone they'd only met that same night?

She wrestled with the ropes again, but if anything it only seemed to make them tighter.

In the distance she could hear a loud rumble, like an earthquake rippling towards her. . .

Great puffs of black smoke told Cuthbert he'd reached the engine. A set of steep iron steps led down to where a large brown bear stood on the fireman's plate, steering. He looked around for his sister, but his view was hidden by the smoke and steam. There was no time to wait. . .

Macabre's training methods had left the giant beast with scars both mental and physical: large patches bare of fur, some missing teeth, and an exceedingly bad temper. Cuthbert knew the bear of old, knew that he would have to tread very carefully indeed. Smoke, rising in clouds from the boiler, gave him a little cover. He could see the brake lever that would halt the locomotive. Hooking his feet into the top of the ladder which lead from the roof, Cuthbert dangled upside down until his hands were just a few centimetres away from the lever. He stretched further, felt the ice-cold metal of the brakes, and began to pull. The lever clanked as it began to move. Unfortunately this alerted the bear, and it span round. He gave the lever another hard tug. This time it didn't move at all.

Now Cuthbert could feel the hot breath of the bear as it bore down upon him, teeth bared, a low, angry rumble in its chest.

The beast already had hold of his hands. A desperate struggle began. As the bear dragged its pale, skinny adversary from the metal steps and held him helplessly in mid-air, it looked as if he was going to throw Cuthbert from the train.

Cuthbert's legs wriggled, as he squirmed and struggled. "Get off me, you brute!"

Now they were both standing over the metal footplate connecting the train to the rest of the carriages, but it was still the bear who had the advantage. . .

"Gggggg," was all Cuthbert could say, as his face turned blue. Little by little the life was being squeezed out of poor Cuthbert. And being so small and frail there wasn't a great deal to squeeze out. . .

Things began to blur. He made one last grab for the brake lever, then closed his eyes and waited for the end to come. . .

Lisa was waiting for the end too. The whole frame of the roller coaster was shaking now, groaning under the weight of the advancing train. Her head was filled with terrible sounds. Grinding screaming metal, a shrill whistle, the smell of acrid smoke filling the air. . .

TSSSSSCHHHH!

Lisa began saying her prayers and making her peace with the world. Her final thoughts were what a mess the train would make of Les's hire-costume. There was a judder along the rails, she sensed the shadow of that train not a carriage length away. . .

237

All was steam and fog and confusion. Fatima's sudden presence caused the bear to release his grip on Cuthbert and he swiped angrily at her with his paw. Cuthbert slowly recovered his senses.

"Fatima!"

The bear gave a loud, threatening growl, and lunged towards Fatima, claws bared, teeth exposed. She felt a large paw, and then long, scratching nails around her throat. Things looked black indeed when. . .

CLANG!

There was a dull, metallic thud, followed by an off-key, wobbly, vibrating sound, like a giant tuning fork. The bear driver stood absolutely still for a second and then fell to the ground. He was out cold.

Fatima looked up and saw Cuthbert standing holding the fireman's shovel.

Fatima, jumping down from the roof, grabbed at the brake lever and tugged hard.

Tsssch! . . .Clank. . . Tsssch! . . .Clank. . . Tssssssch!

When she looked up again she saw a large smile etched across her brother's pale features.

"You did it!"

The Carnival Train suddenly shook, as though it had been hit by lightning, and then began to slow. Sparks flew upwards into the greyblue gloom. Carriages knocked into one another, wheels span, suitcases fell from luggage compartments, and the giant brown bear released its grip on Cuthbert.

"What's happening?" squawked Macabre from underneath Mr Spangly (who'd fallen on top of him).

"I think we ran over the police lady!" sobbed the tearful clown.

But the Carnival Train had come to a halt just a couple of metres from where Lisa remained tied to the line.

CHAPTER SIXTY-FIVE

An Unexpected Stop

Macabre hurried to the window, yanking angrily at the emergency cord. "What's happening?" he shouted. And then, as was his habit, shouted exactly the same thing again, only twice as loudly, and with twice the venom, "WHAT'S HAPPENING?"

"We're still stopped," answered Mr Spangly, who liked to state the obvious.

"Why?" replied Macabre, his expression growing darker still.

Now Mr Spangly was struggling. He couldn't really think of a good reason. "Perhaps there's a station?"

Macabre's tiny store of patience snapped. He grabbed Mr Spangly by the lapels and threw him the length of the carriage, his fall broken only by the Brothers Fantoni, who had just entered the carriage. All three collapsed like ninepins.

"A station?" bellowed Macabre. "There's not going to be a station on a roller-coaster ride, is there?"

"No," sobbed Mr Spangly. "It must be something else."

"The Gruesome Twosome are behind this! Our trap

has snapped shut at last! Quick! To the engine!"
snarled the chief, and he and his crack troops set off
through the cramped carriages as fast as their very
large feet would carry them. . .

Fatima gave her brother a big hug. It was quite a
moment. But only a moment, for Lisa Palermo still lay
tied to the line, waiting for a train. . .

Not for long. The Gruesome Twosome sprinted to
where she lay and with nimble fingers had soon
unpicked the ropes binding her.

The three friends indulged in a brief but magical
embrace.

"Thank you, thank you," rejoiced Lisa.

"You are our friend," answered Fatima, before
breaking off at the sound of an approaching commo-
tion.

"Macabre!" cried Cuthbert, in terror.

Lisa turned defiantly towards the train behind
them. "You two go, I can hold them off. . ."

Fatima shook her head. "No, Lisa. Once we were
two, now we are three."

"We escape together, or not at all," added
Cuthbert. For the merest moment the three friends
took in the sense of what that meant. They were
together or they were nothing.

Cuthbert, Fatima, and Lisa stood at the top of the
roller-coaster ride, half frozen with fear, wondering
what to do next. The grinning face of the Circus Train
stared back at them down the line: a bear with a sore

241

head was just coming round on the footplate of the engine; Macabre and his Circus Army were swarming through the carriages. This was the scene that Halloween night as the mist began to fade and the moon began to pale. . .

Macabre was no fool. He knew his plan was unravelling. The ship would soon be setting sail for the East and still the best act in his show had not been recaptured. He stood in the engine compartment with wild eyes and dark thoughts.

"Time is running out and so is my patience!" He cracked his whip with such fury it sounded like gunshot.

CHAPTER SIXTY-SIX

When the Witch's Spell Breaks, the Railway Will Rock

Seconds counting down, falling, like snowflakes, like autumn leaves, like the faces of the crowd by the merry-go-round. Badhagg felt every second pass, counted it in the dusty attic of her mind. Ticktock ticktock, counting down. Ticktock, not long now. . .

Badhagg found herself alone in the carriage as everyone else had raced to the front of the engine.

In her hand she was clutching a piece of faded parchment, dated twenty years previously.

Head in the lion's mouth.

A debt paid.

Dark memories now banished.

The midnight moon shone down on the fragile parchment and right on cue, dissolved it into dust as though it were a thousand years old and not merely two times ten.

The witch, Badhagg, was free. Her bond to Macabre was no more.

"Heeheeheeheeheeheee!"

The pleasure of being able to use her witch's powers for herself alone poured in upon her. A reviving stream of magic. Laughlikeabanshee, echoing into the night. To her delight and amazement, the first thing the witch spied in her new found freedom was her favourite flying broom, the *Skycruiser II*.

"Perfect!" Her thoughts turned at once to what mischief she might do to Macabre and his circus crew. "Revenge tastes sweeter than frogspawn!" she cackled.

Capturing Cuthbert and Fatima was no longer her concern, replaced instead by a burning desire to punish Macabre for his cruel deeds during twenty long years.

As a first step she resolved to lift the spell that she had placed upon the unfortunate populace of Windflower. The witch began to chant strange words. Backward sentences, resounding out across the fairground. This raising of the spell reached the ears of those imprisoned on the Carnival Train itself. Staring, flyingsaucer eyes took on their normal appearance once again (except for little Jimmy Nomark's, whose eyes were that way anyhow). Sheriff Cohnberg, Cornershop Les, the local schoolkids, Ophelia Hook the town beauty; all came slowly back to life, yawning and stretching as though awakened from a long sleep.

"What's goin' on?"

"What is this place?"

"Hey – it's the fairgound!"

Badhagg, standing now on the roof of the train with arms aloft, gave a satisfied but shrill laugh and mounted her broom. "Broom be swift, broom be true. Take me away from this performing zoo!"

The engine roared. The throttle opened. A cloud of pinkish-blue smoke billowed up. VAROOOOM! Badhagg was gone, up into the Halloween night.

A first, faint star peeked through the thin veil of cloud. . .

The evil ringmaster and his henchmen were surprised to see the bear lying on the footplate, rubbing its head. The engine was still completely motionless.

"Asleep on the job! Throw him to the lions!"

The poor bear was carted off by two clowns in suits before it could even explain what had happened.

"Badhagg? Where's Badhagg?" roared the ring-master, angrily. "I need a spell from that old crone!"

"I saw her shoot by on her broom!" answered Mr Spangly, when it became clear that no one else was going to risk a reply.

"Defying orders, eh? Well she'll pay for that, oh riddle-me, yes – you'll all pay!" he thundered. "And why has this train stopped?"

"Zee young lady eez gone!" gasped the Bearded Lady, glancing at the empty track up ahead.

"Zee line is bare," she gasped in her Parisian accent. "Zere is only rope. *Oh mais non!*"

Macabre let out a roar that could be heard in nearby Greed (pop:214). "WHAAAAAAT! I can't believe this. Why is everyone trying to ruin me? Send for the lions! Call forth the Circus Army! This is war!"

In all his years of fear, Mr Spangly had never been so frightened of his master as he was in those moments. Tears trundled down his snowy-white cheeks and he shuddered silently at the thought of the fate awaiting Cuthbert and Fatima and their police-woman friend. . .

CHAPTER SIXTY-SEVEN

Going Down

Lisa and the Gruesome Twosome had decided their only course of action was to climb back down the timber frame of the ride as fast as possible. Lisa hesitated as she looked over the edge. The mist was clearing and the darkness of that terrible Halloween night was about to be replaced by a chill, glittering dawn. The lights of the fairground now stood out against a seagrey sky.

"Come on, Lisa!" shouted Fatima. "No time to lose!"

Lisa hesitated again. It was such a long way down. She didn't feel strong enough for a climb of this magnitude. Or brave enough. But with Macabre's angry army about to steam down the track towards them, there really was no alternative. Trembling hands reached out for the first timber. There a terrifying view of a three hundred foot drop. Wind whistled in black hair. Still the tracks vibrated with the motion of the train's recent, juddering halt.

Dangling precariously at first, Lisa fought to find a first tentative foothold, then guided by the twins, moved along the slippery beams until she could crouch alongside them and help plot their next move.

CHAPTER SIXTY-EIGHT

Octavia the trapeze girl
mistress of the backward flip
somersaulted out of the circus tent
and off on to an ocean ship.

Meanwhile the Carnival Train, her brake-lever finally released, had set off again, with two penguins shovelling furiously to feed her hungry boilers.

Macabre stared out along the tracks, forced to hold on to his top hat, moustache flowing in the speed-induced breeze.

"When we get them, they'll be sorry! What horrors I shall devise! No one defies the Great Macabre and gets away with it!"

"Except Octavia, the albino Trapeze Girl," added Mr Spangly.

Macabre's face underwent a horrible change.

Mr Spangly realized at once what a big mistake he'd made, and frantically tried to dig his way out of the hole. "I'm sorry, ringmaster, sir. I . . . I . . . I didn't mean to mention. . ."

Macabre turned and lashed out at the sequin-suited

clown, causing him to fall from the footplate of the train, from whence he plummeted with an ear-piercing scream. Down past timber supports, past giant letters, past the Gruesome Twosome and Lisa slowly climbing down the ride. . .

"AAAAAAAAAAAAAAARGH!"

His landing, many seconds later, was signalled by a plaintive and terminal hoot of his horn. Poor Mr Spangly!

"Anyone else got anything to say?" asked the ring-master, eyes flitting across the faces of his henchmen for signs of dissent. There was a moment of silence before one of the clowns, a plump figure with a spot-ted kipper tie, raised his hand.

"Well?"

The clown was sweating profusely. "I . . . th-th-think th-th-they're c-climbing back d-down the roller-coaster, sir." The funnyman was holding Lisa's police badge, which she'd left behind in the carriage.

Macabre snatched the badge, examined it briefly, and then flung it overboard, in much the same way he'd cast aside poor Mr Spangly. "We can still catch them before the ship sails!"

He gave a crack of his whip, summoning the fiercest poodles and the hungriest lions from their carriages.

And for the first time, the evil seals were ordered forth, spinning rubber beach balls on their noses, wad-dling fiercely through the throng of crowded carriages. An aroma of seaweed and sulphur filling the air.

"No one loves the circus any more!" cried Macabre

to his assembled troops. "They drive us from town to town, and what do they care of the magical arts of which we are masters? Nothing! Empty seats and empty hearts, that's what the future holds for us, unless we win this fight!"

Size twenty shoes stamped their approval.

"So bring me the Gruesome Twosome and their meddlesome mate. Then at last we can board the Maharajah's boat and set sail for pastures anew!"

Macabre laughed and the ranks of the Circus Army laughed too. The Carnival Train had reached the top of the circuit and had begun to plunge downwards, faster and faster, like a falling acrobat.

CHAPTER SIXTY-NINE

**TRANSCRIPT OF RADIO MESSAGE
RECEIVED BY WINDFLOWER POLICE HQ**

"Hi, Bill, this is Sheriff Cohnberg."

"Harry! Where you bin?"

"Long story, Bill, long story. . ."

"It always is, you old dog."

"Listen, buddy, I need some back-up up at the fairground."

"The fairground? Whad'ya doin' there this time o' night?"

"I'm tryin' to win a coconut, whaddya think? Now get me some back-up will ya?"

"Roger. No need to shout, Harry, I still got my hearing."

"I want my mum!" shouted Hercules.

"Quiet, kid!" countered Abel Doodlebug, school bus driver. Both were amazed to have found themselves seated on the Big Wheel, which had long since stopped turning, and was creaking faintly in the breeze but not moving an inch.

"Will ya both shut up!" roared the sheriff, trying to use his radio. "I'm tryin' to get us outta this mess!"

Beneath them, the great mass of townsfolk were also waking from the spell and slowly becoming aware of their situation: kids found themselves far from home, candyfloss in hand; adults were amazed to find themselves riding the Whirlitzer or Big Dipper. They woke, yawning and stretching, trying hard to remember how or why they were here. The younger and more nervous children had begun to sob or wail according to personal preference.

Abel Doodlebug decided he would never drive a school bus again as long as he lived.

Yet, while others woke, Barrabas O'Hanlon still lay in a heap beside the upturned dodgem, Blackdog crouched forlornly by his side. There was no sign of life.

Lisa, Cuthbert, and Fatima were still descending the huge, creaky, timber frame of the roller-coaster ride. As the Carnival Train passed overhead they could just make out Macabre, angrily cracking his whip, and hear, growing ever fainter, the roar of lions, poodles, and cannon. Cannon?

Yes. Macabre's parting shot whistled overhead, before exploding in a puff of black, acrid smoke.

"Will he never give up?" mused Lisa, the Carnival Train almost out of sight now as it accelerated towards the down-slope of the figure of eight circuit.

"No," answered Cuthbert. "We must proceed with haste!"

Macabre, indeed, was far from beaten. "Don't worry, my friends. As mother used to say, 'Life is a roller-coaster ride. A loop the loop'. We'll catch them soon enough!"

He gave a throaty chuckle, like an evil pantomime villain.

"Just one small flaw, chief," interrupted one of the penguins.

"What's that?"

"We don't have a driver!"

Macabre thought about this for a moment, before realizing to his horror that it was true.

"Action stations," he cried, with goggle eyes. "To the engine! We need to find a driver fast! Get to it! Where is Mr Spangly?"

Macabre paused, remembering the recent fate of his right hand clown.

"Curse that foolish funnyman: when finally we could use him he's not around!"

With that, Macabre's army raced back towards the engine, huffing and puffing through the carriages, and as they ran, ice-cold wind lashed their faces, and they were covered in clouds of pitch black steam, for the Carnival Train had reached full speed. So high a speed indeed, that rivets were popping from her funnel, and her wheels barely touched the tracks. Disaster seemed certain, at the end of the line. . .

CHAPTER SEVENTY

"KIDNAPPED!"
BY HERCULES INKBLOT, AGED 8.

I used to like trains, specially when they came through our town and all the folks would go runnin up to the station jus to see who had come but not now. mother said it was the evil clowns that came our way by train and then they cast a spell mother says she wishes she cood do that with me and dad sometimes, trains are very frightening and next time mother says I have to take the bus.

Into view flew a black silhouette. Too large to be a bird, too small for a plane. Badhagg the witch it was, astride her broom, cloak billowing behind, her thoughts still turned towards the evil Macabre and how she might be revenged.

"Twenty long years I've waited for this. Twenty years!" So saying, she took her broom into a steep, bone-juddering dive, heading at full speed towards the Carnival Train. Peering down, one arm raised, bony fingers pointing, she muttered an eerie incantation:

Carnival Train, it's time
you left the track.
Time you quit this town
and never came back!

Her straggly locks blew behind her like a tangle of seaweed, the chill air sucked in her haggard cheeks as Badhagg continued spitting out her rhyme:

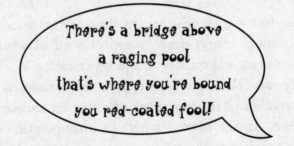

There's a bridge above
a raging pool
that's where you're bound
you red-coated fool!

The Carnival Train was bathed, for a moment, in a strange amber-coloured light, at which point it suddenly left the rails of the roller-coaster ride, and began to fly through the air.

Badhagg uttered an evil, cackling laugh, and took her broom alongside the locomotive for a closer look. . .

Macabre had felt the strange dislocation of the witch's spell and the sudden flight into mid-air.

"What's happening?" he snarled, clutching the side of the compartment in an attempt to keep his balance.

"Ve haf left the tracks!" answered the Remarkable Otto, still trapped in the window, but with a splendid view of the town below. "Ve are traffelling too fast!"

The ringmaster still hadn't spotted Badhagg, her broom now flying alongside the opposite window. She waved her hands again, and this time sent the train spinning down until it landed snugly on the rails of the main line from Windflower to Foghorn as it wound its way along the cliff-tops.

Macabre smiled. Green sharpasshark'steeth. "That's better!"

But he was premature in his celebrations. An explosion of bright sparks was followed by a furious clicketyclack of grinding, buckling track.

"Ve are still going too quickly!" shouted the Remarkable Otto, brows bulging, sea breeze stinging his eyes. In the carriages behind him, poodles were being thrown to the ground, balancing seals dropped their balls, and the Circus Army fell into disarray.

For the first time that anyone could remember, the great Finian Macabre fell silent and, as the train rattled crazily on, he said nothing.

CHAPTER SEVENTY-ONE

THE TESTIMONY OF OPHELIA HOOK (19)

It was like I had closed my eyes and gone into some strange dream, exceptin this weren't no dream, no, cos when I came to there was Sheriff Cohnberg and Les from the general store and a whole lotta other folk from the town. Just what happened to us no one knew, but it seems it wuz all to do with that train I seen in the front street, and some circus they say has had us all bamboozled and in a hex.

Lisa couldn't believe what she had just witnessed. "Did you see what happened to the rest of the Carnival Train?"

"Fortune has smiled on us at last!" answered Cuthbert, leaping to the ground with an athletic tumble.

"The witch Badhagg has had a hand in these events, methinks," he continued. "I spied her broom flying high."

Fatima nodded. "She has turned against Macabre at last."

"Would she do that?" asked Lisa, slightly incredulous.

"We may never know," replied Fatima. "But if he has fallen foul of Badhagg then he had better beware, for dark magic can easily be turned upon those who have used it for themselves."

"Swell," smiled Lisa, climbing carefully down from the last remaining timber. "That's the best news I've heard in a long time! Hey! There's the sheriff!"

The lawman in question was overhead, still trapped on the Big Wheel. Lisa ran over to the controls, and switched the ride back on again. After a pause the giant structure ground back into life. All around them the townsfolk continued to revive after their ordeal.

"Cuthbert, Fatima! It looks like the spell has been broken!"

Cuthbert and Fatima exchanged a subdued look. They weren't too sure how things would work out now. What if the townsfolk blamed them for what had happened? They were from the circus after all – and they'd run away from Sheriff Cohnberg – and whoever believes runaways? No one!

Lisa saw the twins try to melt away and caught hold of them just in time. "Hey, guys, what's the rush?"

Sad, dark eyes looked up, filled with fear.

"I want everyone to know how you saved them," continued Lisa. "You two are heroes!"

"Knife-throwers," mumbled Cuthbert. "Unemployed knife-throwers."

Lisa told them to stay there while she went to help the still-confused passengers disembark from the Big Wheel. Some of her kids were there and she greeted them with unrestrained relief.

Sheriff Cohnberg was also on hand. "Miss Palermo, am I glad to see you!" Before he could say anything else, his radio crackled into life and he was distracted by urgent police business. "That you, Harry? What the deuce is happenin'? I had your wife on the phone. She ain't happy, says you ain't been home all night – you'd better start makin' a white flag!"

From behind him emerged the rest of the townspeople who'd been trapped on the Big Wheel, dazed, confused, nervously jabbering, or laughing like fools without knowing why, or else like Les the shopkeeper, stunned and silent, still half-asleep.

Cuthbert and Fatima now took their opportunity to slip away. They had no wish to be heroes, no desire to be caught in the glow of the spotlight ever again. . . .

Lisa caught up with them just as they'd reached the gates of the fairground, and were on the point of climbing back on to their pogo-sticks.

"Hey!" she shouted, still dressed in her cop costume. "Where are you guys going?"

"To see Mrs Hubbard," answered Fatima. "We must tell her that we are safe."

"You're right," agreed Lisa. "How could I have forgotten? Mind if I tag along?"

Cuthbert and Fatima didn't mind at all. If there

was one person they now trusted in all the world, it was Lisa Palermo.

A faint dawn, soft as candlelight now glimmered on the horizon. The journey to Gravestone Walk seemed short indeed after all that had gone before.

CHAPTER SEVENTY-TWO

The Carnival Train, steaming and gyrating, raced on towards its fate.

A bridge appeared up ahead. This was the famous Doodlebug Viaduct (mentioned in several guidebooks to the area), built to connect the two small towns of Greed and Foghorn. Nobody knew why anyone would want to connect two such small and dreary towns, but in 18—— work began, and by the following fall, the first train had rolled over the dizzyingly high, single-line, timber-framed bridge, to be met by home made flags and an enthusiastic anthem sung by local school children. *"Welcome train and brave explorers, welcome none and all to Foghorn's borders, hoorah!"*

But we digress. Back on the Carnival Train, still under the influence of witchcraft, even the perfectly balanced Fantoni Brothers could hardly stay on their feet. Macabre, knowing he could never beat Badhagg now the twenty-year bond was over, had abandoned hope and sat crouched in a corner, pulling the rim of his top hat lower and lower until it covered his ears and eyes. It was as if all the fight had suddenly gone out of him.

The Maharajah's boat would sail without them.

The Gruesome Twosome had escaped for good. Mother was right. "You'll never run a circus, you've scarecrow straw for brains!" Like a giant, deflated balloon, Macabre was no more.

All around him was the frantic hooting of clown horns, the worried bark of fearful poodles. Without their leader the Circus Army was nothing.

The Doodlebug Viaduct flashed into view. Beneath it, the waters raged and bubbled, licking angrily against century-old timbers. The train clattered overhead and its noise sang down the wooden supports. Badhagg, flying alongside, pointed a gnarled finger once more:

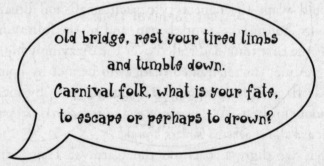

old bridge, rest your tired limbs and tumble down.
Carnival folk, what is your fate, to escape or perhaps to drown?

No sooner were the words spoken than the bridge began to twist and shift. Part of it – a length of rail and some timber supports – fell into the turbulent waters. The train raced on, bump and grind, towards the gaping precipice. . .

Too late the brakes, too late the clowns' horns honking for all they were worth. . .

The corridors were now packed with giant feet, jostling penguins, frantic seals all in a desperate panic.

"No one loves the circus any more," sobbed Macabre, a broken figure. "No one loves the circus any more. . ."

With a scream like a million amateur violins, the Carnival Train crashed over the edge of the broken-backed bridge, only to freeze, impossibly, in mid-air.

Badhagg gave another chuckle, and then a victory roll on her favourite broom.

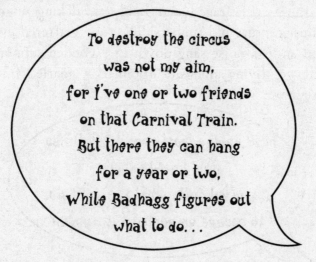

To destroy the circus
was not my aim,
for I've one or two friends
on that Carnival Train.
But there they can hang
for a year or two,
While Badhagg figures out
what to do. . .

Closer to the train she soared, until she could see the Remarkable Otto, his head now looking directly down at the raging river, body still trapped inside the mid-air frozen train.

"I'll be back next Halloween!" screeched Badhagg, who'd always had a soft spot for the big man. "Or maybe not!"

And with that she turned her broom again and roared off towards the brightening horizon.

The Carnival Train dangled in mid-air, half on the bridge and half off. The only sound was the rushing of the river below, and the last blasts of steam from her cooling engines.

The Great Macabre and his army were too frightened to speak and too frightened to move. They would have to wait for the witch's return, however long that might take. . .

CHAPTER SEVENTY-THREE

Blueberry pie,
Blueberry pie,
Won't you try some
blueberry pie?

Local song, Windflower.

22a Gravestone Walk looked different in daylight: not so ramshackle and not so frightening. The same couldn't be said for Cuthbert and Fatima, who still resembled two little ghosts who'd somehow strayed in from the nearby graveyard.

Mrs Hubbard opened the door and smothered them with kisses and hugs. "Won't you stay for blueberry pie, my pretty marionettes?"

"Yeah," added Lisa, who had accompanied them there. "You'll have to stick around now – Windflower's your home."

"Home?" Fatima liked the sound of the word.

"Home on the range." Cuthbert liked it too. "Only one problem, dear friends. . ."

Lisa and Mrs Hubbard both looked suddenly troubled.

"We would like to learn more of our true origins. There are questions we have to answer. If we aren't from here and we weren't from there, then *where?*"

Fatima nodded her head in agreement. "There is still much to learn. But wherever we roam, Windflower is our second home. . ."

Mrs Hubbard's soft snowflake eyes welled up like a mountain lake in spring. "Oh really, my sweethearts, you can't go off, just like that, without a plan or even a picnic basket. . ."

And it did seem odd that the Gruesome Twosome having searched for so long for somewhere to rest, and having found it, should decide so quickly to move on again. But once a thought takes hold inside your soul, it can be impossible to ignore.

Lisa laid a gentle arm around the old lady's frail shoulders. "I think we're wasting our breath, Mrs Hubbard. When the Gruesome Twosome make up their minds to do something, it gets done. Right, guys?"

Cuthbert and Fatima smiled.

Lisa was trying hard to hide the tears welling up inside. "I'll walk with you as far as the crossroads."

"That would be nice, thank you."

Mrs Hubbard pulled her shawl tightly about her. "Won't you at least stay till spring?"

"We will return, one day, dear old Mrs Hubbard," answered Fatima, giving her a kiss.

"You have been a true friend," added Cuthbert, who never kissed anyone.

So it was that Lisa and the Gruesome Twosome retreated back down the winding overgrown footpath until Mrs Hubbard's frail figure was no more than a speck in the distance.

Once at the crossroads it was time for more farewells.

"Back to boring reality I guess," sniffed Lisa, who hadn't felt sad at saying goodbye to children for a very long time. But then, she'd never met kids quite like Cuthbert and Fatima.

"You two take care now."

"We will."

"And if you ever need me, you know where I am."

"We know."

"'Cept I won't be dressed as a cop next time!"

"Adieu, fair Lisa," waved Cuthbert.

"Don't cry," added Fatima, though she felt like crying herself. "We'll meet again!"

"I wonder," sniffed Lisa to herself. "I wonder. . ."

CHAPTER SEVENTY-FOUR

The Carnival is Over

Barrabas rubbed his head and blinked his eyes: the sun was bright and hurt them. He could hear nothing but silence. What time was it? Where was he? His eyes focused first on the telescope lying on the ground beside him, or rather what remained of his telescope.

It had been crushed into tiny pieces. The sight of this made him remember the night before. A flash of chrome, a sudden collision. . .

Then he saw Blackdog. Seeing his master miraculously restored to life, the sad and weary-looking mongrel bounded to Barrabas's side and began licking his face and hands with unconfined joy.

"Easy, easy," smiled the lighthouse keeper.

The fairground was deserted, empty of life except for the lighthouse keeper, now on his feet, rubbing his head, feeling a cut lip and bruised bones.

He glanced up at the roller-coaster ride in whose huge shadow he now stood. The train he thought he'd seen was no longer there. And what about the young lady tied to the line? No sign of her either. Barrabas felt as if he'd been asleep for a year or more.

But this was only the morning after. He could still smell candyfloss and toffee apples.

Cuthbert and Fatima had been at this Halloween fair, he knew that with a father's instincts. But where were they now?

He climbed quickly to his feet, brushing himself down. His lip tasted of dried blood and his hands and arms were grazed. No matter.

The dodgem car that had knocked him to the ground still lay there, overturned, with a large dent in its shiny chrome bumper. Where was the clown that had been driving it? *Where were any of the clowns?* And the ringmaster known as Macabre that he had yet to meet?

Blackdog was still celebrating his master's return to the land of the living. He ran round and round in excited circles. And then, when quite sure Barrabas was fully restored to health, he began barking.

"What is it, boy? Where do you want me to go?"

Blackdog was running towards the gates of the fairground and then racing back as if to encourage his master to follow.

Barrabas took the hint and began walking after his canine companion. Together they soon reached the fairground gates, Barrabas's giant strides eating up the ground as he strove to keep up with Blackdog.

"Are they still in town, boy? Is that what you're trying to tell me? Maybe we can catch them yet?" And so saying he broke into a run, hurrying past deflated black balloons and forgotten popcorn and motionless rides.

Blackdog and Barrabas continued down the road, heading swiftly back towards the town.

Heading in the opposite direction at that very same moment, was another figure, moving equally purposefully. A young woman with long black hair, tired eyes, and a crumpled policewoman's uniform.

Barrabas spotted her at once and reached instinctively for the picture in his pocket. How many thousands of times had that image been shown? Its edges were worn now, and the tones of the picture fading.

Blackdog was barking excitedly.

"Excuse me, miss," began Barrabas. "I wonder have you ever, in your travels, come across two tiny tots who look like this? Except by now they would be ten years older?"

Lisa looked at the picture and her heart leaped. She then looked again at Barrabas, somewhat bedraggled in appearance, stubble on his face, cut lip, kindly eyes blinking in the dawn, and wondered if she could trust this stranger. The family resemblance seemed to her very strong, even across the years. And why else would he have a picture of her friends as young babies? Blackdog fixed Lisa with a sorrowful gaze.

"Are you . . . are you by any chance their father?" she asked the lighthouse keeper.

Barrabas nodded, still not daring to hope.

"I am." He paused, hardly able to speak. "Have you seen them? My Cuthbert and Fatima?"

"Yes . . . yes . . . I've just left them."

Barrabas's eyes filled with light and hope.

"They were heading towards the coast," continued Lisa, breathlessly. "I can take you there. I'm sure we'll catch them up. They can't have got far. This is incredible. I can't believe you were really here, all along!"

Barrabas smiled and though he had a thousand things to say, nothing came out. But Lisa could see his joy and Blackdog sensed it too, as he barked twice, loudly, and then turned and started running towards the sea. Barrabas and Lisa were right behind him.

Back on the open road, the Gruesome Twosome were making good progress.

"I think," said Cuthbert, after they'd been travelling for quite a while, "freedom tastes even sweeter than one of Mrs Hubbard's blueberry pies. . ."

And they continued to pogo on towards the coastline, just as a great golden sun began to climb above the waves and fill the sky and landscape for miles around with its light.

The End

Have you read

Going Out with a Bang

by Joel Snape?

"I'm not doing it," I said, in my firmest You're-Just-Wasting-Your-Time voice.

"I'm not really asking you to *do* anything, if you don't want to," pointed out Dec.

"I don't want to, and I'm not going to."

"Just come with me."

"No, because I know what's going to happen," I said, stubbornly.

After German, my mind was racing with ways to a) talk to Kate after school, b) appear much cooler/funnier/more attractive than I actually am and c) keep her away from Matt the Idiot. But then it occurred to me – there was no way I was going to do that tonight, after her first day at school. And however persistent Matt the Idiot was, it was unlikely that he was going to get to twang her bra straps, or whatever, that particular evening.

Besides, I didn't *really* know what was going to happen, whatever I told Dec. If I had, I'd definitely have walked off then and there, and not even given him a chance to talk me round. As it was, if we kept walking in the direction of the skatepark, it was only a matter of time.

Bristol skatepark's great. They might not give enough money to schools (according to my mum) or be any good at collecting bins (Dad), but there's one thing I'll say for our council — they know how to build a skatepark. A couple of years ago, they decided that something to keep The Kids out of trouble might be a good idea — and at that point they must have got some lottery money or something, because instead of just sticking a half-pipe in a children's playground, they built this enormous skate-wonderland full of grind rails, vert ramps and funboxes. On Saturdays you can sit there for ages, just watching people pull cool tricks or (even better) slam into things.

It didn't really stop the trouble, of course. The kids who used to skive off school, smoke, drink cider, spraypaint stuff and threaten other kids, didn't stop. Now they all just do it in one place, which is why all the half-pipes are covered in graffiti, the paths are all covered in crisp packets and the grass verges around the park are covered in nutters. That's why the skatepark's fine on a weekend, when there are parents around to watch their kids work on kickflips, but not exactly the greatest place to go after school. None of this matters to Dec, though. He goes there all the time – and he had a plan.

The thing is, though: I can't even skateboard. I had a go once, when I was nine, except that I'd forgotten the golden rule of any sport – if you've never tried it on flat land, *don't try it on the steepest hill in your town.* One pair of ripped trousers and two severely scraped elbows later, and that was it for me and skateboarding.

Dec's much more sensible. He can ollie things, do 50–50 grinds and manage decent manual rolls – hey, I can play Tony Hawk – they're all things he learned to do before skating was *quite* as cool as it is now. And that's enough for him. Ten minutes of serious skating and he's off wandering around and chatting to all the thrasher girls who sit on the grass banks. Which is where I was supposed to come in.

The reason he'd had to dash off on Saturday, Dec explained, was that he'd met a girl on one of his earlier trips to the park. She was really pretty, he thought he was in with a chance, and she had this mate who sort of wouldn't give them any time to themselves, and . . . and it was about that point that I worked out what was going on.

This wasn't Dec setting me up, whatever he said – it was Dec trying to get rid of someone else. And the weird thing about Dec is, he thinks you won't notice when he tries this stuff.

"Look, all you have to do is talk to Natalie's mate for a bit while we go for a walk somewhere. Otherwise I'll never get rid of her."

"Is Natalie's mate pretty?"

"Yeah! Fairly."

"What do you mean, 'fairly'?"

"I think you'll like her."

"Do *you* like her?"

"Not as much as I like Natalie."

Suddenly, I remembered our conversation in the cafe.

"Is she third division?"

"Ha! I'd say she's. . ." Dec gave it a bit of thought. "First division. Just not premier league. It's an easy away win."

"Why didn't you ask Will?"

"Because he's already been relegated."

That carried on right until we were at the skatepark. Worried as I was, I had to admit that I wanted to meet Dec's potential girlfriend – and I couldn't help wondering what her mate would be like. I probably wasn't going to fancy her as much as Kate, or anything, but there was no harm in looking, was there?

"There they are," said Dec, as we walked towards the gates.

Dec pointed at two girls lying together on one of the grass banks. They were both wearing identical black hooded tops and combats, although one of them had brown hair and the other one was blonde. I couldn't really tell what they looked like at that distance – and besides, I didn't know which one was which.

"Come on."

Before I knew it, Dec had taken his school shirt off and stuffed it in his bag. Underneath, he was wearing a T-shirt with some sort of ultra-trendy kung-fu monkey logo on. What with that, his black school trousers and his jacket, he didn't look much different to most of the people skating. And I was still wearing my school uniform. I couldn't believe it. He'd probably been plotting this ever since that little chat in the coffee shop.

"Oh, this is great. Thanks for warning me," I said.

"It'll be fine. Come on."

"Hang on a... No, just stop right... Oh, I don't believe this." I tried to protest, but Dec was already heading straight for them.

Up closer, I started to feel even worse. Both girls were plastered with black mascara, but the blonde one was really pretty — and she was obviously Dec's type. The other one wasn't ugly, exactly, but she was really pale, had a weird smile and . . . well, she looked mad. I don't know what it was — maybe the stupid pink hair extensions, maybe the tatty, fingerless gloves or clump boots — but she just had this aura that said, Danger: Keep Away. They were both giggling at nothing in particular, except that the dangerous-looking one was making a sort of snorting noise while she did it. Eep.

"Natalie, Fiona — this is Dylan," said Dec, stepping forward with his best girl-charming smile firmly in place. Natalie, I figured out, was the blonde one, who smiled at Dec. Fiona was the crazy-looking one, who just scrunched up her nose a bit.

They stopped laughing and sat up to give me deliberately serious looks.

"Pleased to meet you."

"Nice tie."

And both of them exploded into giggles again.

I suppose I could have at least taken the tie off.